When The Side B*tch Understands The Assignment 2

Kevina Hopkins

Miss Jazzie

When The Side B*tch Understands The Assignment 2

Mailing List

To stay up to date on new releases, plus get information on contests, sneak peeks, and more,

Go To The Website Below...

www.colehartsignature.com

Chapter 1
Paris

I had to be in the fucking twilight zone. I only came in here to tell Draco that I was choosing to take the intern position. It would be hands-on and more exposure for me in my profession. I'd stacked enough money off Draco that I wouldn't have to work for the next ten years if I didn't want to. Our time was up, and he was about to find out now whether I was pregnant or not. That's another fucking curve ball I had to deal with. I honestly didn't know who the father was, but I could bet every dollar in my bank account that it was Draco's. He didn't need to know that though.

My heart raced, hands trembled as I watched this bitch hold my sonogram. She had the audacity to actually go through my fucking purse. Alana didn't know how to stay in her fucking lane. I was okay being his side bitch, but the minute I met that bitch, and he made that agreement, sugar was going to turn into shit. We were standing in the office looking at Alana as she held the sonogram in her hand. Draco looked at me with evil slits.

"I see your side bitch pregnant. What the fuck Sasha gon' do when I tell her?" Alana asked with a grin. I jumped at that bitch but Draco pulled me back.

"I don't give a fuck if you tell Sasha or not. You gon' fuck yoself because ain't you and ole girl friends and you fucking her husband too?" I told her, because this bitch was being too dramatic. I came, conquered, and now I was walking away with grace and a whole lotta money, and let's not forget Jonah's sexy ass.

"I fucked the nigga, got his fucking money, and now I'm 'bout to dip out with my money and my baby." I rubbed my barely there stomach as my eyes met Draco's. I rolled my eyes at him with my other hand on my hips because I was over this shit. He made sure the home front was straight, but this bitch Alana had bit off more than she could chew. That nigga looked at me like he wanted to smoke my ass right in his office, but he knew better, or at least I thought he did.

"We both fucking that nigga. He knew the fucking rules coming in this shit. This been going on since yo' young ass was sucking Similac from the fucking bottle," Alana spat, walking closer to me.

"Bitch, you walking up like that first ass whipping didn't damn near kill you. You must be ready for round two." I smirked as she slowly walked over to me. I didn't know what this bitch was about to do, but what she didn't know was that I stayed ready. Before she was inches from me, because I didn't fucking move, Draco snatched her stupid ass up by the front of the short ass dress she had on, and I smirked. My eyes met Draco's and the look of death radiated off them. I knew I'd said too much and would pay for it later. I couldn't spend too much time here because I had Jonah waiting on me at my home. I chose the calmer route and sat my ass on the sofa, crossing my legs, because I didn't want him to yoke me up next.

"Bitch, you really think I give a fuck about you telling Sasha what the fuck I got going on? Go ahead and fucking tell her and I bet she ain't gon' fucking leave me." He waved his ring in front her face and a twinge of jealousy chilled my veins. I didn't know why I was tripping because I knew from the door that he didn't belong to me. He pushed her against the wall with tears falling down her eyes.

"I love you, Draco, but how you chose this young bitch over me?" Alana rolled her eyes at me and I laughed.

"Clearly, he loves this young pussy." I cocked my head to the side and smirked. She rose from the floor like Satan and tried to charge me. I noticed Draco going for his back, which was where his gun was. He pulled it so fast and grabbed Alana by the back of her hair. With his gun to her neck, I jumped when she screamed.

"Bitch, scream again and I'mma blow yo' shit back. You think I give a fuck about your life when you fucking with mine? You open your mouth and you fucking die. Now get the fuck out with dignity or leave with a toe tag," he gritted in her ear, and I almost pissed on myself. I knew Draco could get angry but I'd never witnessed him like that.

"When I let yo' dumbass go, fix yo' fucking face and walk out this bitch and don't look at no fucking body. Leave this bitch with at least half the fucking class you decided to walk in this bitch with." He let her go and put his gun away. I watched as she walked into his private bathroom and cleaned herself up.

How the fuck did she know about that? Had he fucked her in this same office where I rode his dick, on the very sofa I was sitting on? Did he fuck her on the desk that he fucked me doggystyle on? The thoughts running rampant through my mind made my stomach jump. I felt the vomit rising in my throat.

"Give me the trashcan, Draco," I barely got out, but he heard me.

I grabbed the can from him and vomited the nothing I had in my stomach. It looked like water mixed with green shit. It had to be the salad I ate yesterday. I dry heaved until tears came down my cheeks. I felt Draco pulling my hair out the way and moved from his touch. Not because I didn't want him touching me but because my hormones were a raging bull and I wanted to fuck him. I felt my pussy leaking through my bottoms and knew I had to get away from this nigga because I had Jonah waiting for me, and I couldn't go back home smelling like sex. I looked up past Draco and noticed Alana coming out the bathroom fixing her dress, and my blood boiled. My pussy got dry as the Sahara Desert looking at her. Draco noticed where my attention was and turned to give Alana a dirty look.

"Remember what I said, bitch. I'll be in contact," he told her, and she nodded her head before walking out the door. We both sat silent. I'm guessing he was trying to listen if she was going to say anything. When we heard the door shut he stood up, taking the can with him and closing his office door. I sat back on the sofa trying to get my breathing under control. I felt like shit. My body was weak because all I did was vomit. I couldn't wait for this shit to be over and this was just the beginning. I closed my eyes but felt Draco standing before me.

"Now what the fuck was that you were saying when you walked in here?" He was mad but I didn't give a fuck. I didn't say anything. Something about the way he stood before me rocking from side to side with his arms folded had me in a frenzy. Instead of answering him, I pushed my upper body forward and started to unbuckle his belt. My mouth was watering to suck his dick. When I got to the button of his jeans, he grabbed my hands and hissed.

"Nah, we not doing this. What the fuck is going on, Paris?"

I could tell he was struggling because he knew my mouth was lethal. I yanked my hands away from his and stood to my feet.

"I came to tell you that I only need to work weekends

because I'm about to start my internship," I paused, "Oh, and you already know since yo' hoe opened her dick suckers, I'm pregnant," I told him, walking away from him. I had no more to say. I almost slipped but Jonah was too good of a man for me to fuck over. Especially for a nigga that's already married.

"You having my baby?" He smiled from ear to ear. I couldn't rain on his parade and tell him that I didn't know who the father was because I'd fucked Jonah without protection. I just smiled and I guess that was enough for him. He slowly walked toward me, backing me against his desk. His hands rubbed my little belly.

His hands glided up to my nipples and turned them in between his index and thumb. My head fell back as he kissed all over my stomach. He massaged my breasts just the way I liked it, causing a moan to escape my mouth. I knew this shit was wrong but Draco knew my body better than I did. He knew where to touch, kiss, and suck to make a bitch give in, and that's exactly what I was doing and I couldn't stop it. He lifted me up, sitting me on his desk. He unbuttoned my dress and yanked my thong off. He walked between my legs and grabbed the back of my neck for a kiss.

"Did you fuck that bitch in this office? She was very familiar with where the fuck the bathroom was," I asked him as I felt his fingers graze my clit. He looked at me hard.

"Fuck no, the bitch only knew where the shit was because her people helped with the construction."

He pecked my lips before pulling his dick out. I didn't know whether to believe him or not but in that moment, all that shit went out the window. I couldn't be mad because I was his side bitch too, and I wanted some dick. I'd worry about Jonah later. I sat on his desk with my legs wide open, pussy on full display.

"Damn, she juicy." He kneeled down to get a better view. I

sucked on my finger, anticipating his next move. I felt him tongue kissing then nipping at my inner thighs right by my lower lips and he knew that gesture drove me insane. I started to scoot closer to the end of the desk so he could eat the main course.

"Patience, Paris. I need to savor this shit because I know you 'bout to ghost a nigga," he groaned as he bit my other thigh. This wasn't goodbye sex, more like I gotta let you go sex. I grabbed the back of his head, forcing his mouth to my pussy, and he laughed.

"You pushing my head gon' make me go even slower." His breath was making my clit jump. My pussy was a leaking faucet, slob was coming out my mouth. His tongue licked my clit and I shivered.

"Oh my goooodddd," I moaned out loud as he put his entire face in my pussy. He licked and slurped my pussy like it was going out of style. His fingers slid past my clit to my walls.

"Damn, this pussy juicy," he hummed in my shit, and my clit jumped. The tip of his tongue tickled the tip of my clit, intensifying my orgasm.

"I wanna nut on your dick, Dray," I moaned out as he stood to his feet. I watched as he pulled his dick out and stroked it. He tapped the tip against my clit and my legs opened wider.

"Yeah, keep them legs just like that," he said as he stuck the head in.

"Fuck, why yo' shit so tight and wet? This gotta be what pregnant pussy feel like," he mumbled, sliding in inch by inch. Once he hit the bottom, I felt his knees buckle. Then it hit me. This nigga ain't have no children, but that wasn't my problem. He had a wife. That bitch better give him one.

"Pick me up, Dray," I told him, and he did. He fell back on the sofa with me on top. I sat down all the way on his dick and didn't move.

"If yo' lil' ass don't move, I'mma nut, P." His voice was strained with sex. I rolled my hips to a slow beat as he grabbed my hips, pressing his fingers into my ass hard. He palmed them and opened them up to dive deeper.

"Shit." My head fell back as I felt his hand slide from my neck down the middle of my body. I started moving faster, riding him harder. He gripped my hip tighter. My feet planted on each side of him as I went in for the kill. With his index finger in my mouth, I suckled it and bounced my ass all over his dick. I knew he couldn't handle it. He tried to control my movements, but I was too wild for him. All he could do was sit back and enjoy the ride.

"The fuck, P, why you fucking a nigga like that fa? You trying to leave a nigga?" he asked, and I ignored his question because I didn't know what the future held for my life.

"Nah Daddy, I'm trying to make you nut in this pussy." I felt his dick thump inside of me and knew he was about to nut and so was I. I bounced up and down until I drained him dry and my nut was all over him. I leaned over on him out of breath and sat there with his dick still inside of me.

After ten minutes I lifted myself off him and went into the bathroom to take a quick shower and re-dress. Fuck the thong because I barely wore them anyway. After I dressed I walked out the bathroom to a waiting Draco. He looked me up and down.

"Don't fucking leave this room," he said before walking into the bathroom, not bothering to close the door. After he cleaned up he walked out and leaned against his desk. By that time I was dressed with my purse and keys in my hand, ready to get back to Jonah.

"What's up?" I asked him nonchalantly because I knew he hated that.

"Let's address the big fucking elephant in the room. Is that my baby or that lame ass nigga Jonah's?" he asked, walking into my personal space. I wanted to back down but I didn't because I wasn't scared of his ass.

"Nah, this for Jonah," I answered him without a smile.

"So you been fucking him while you were fucking me?!" he said as I walked away from him.

"Yeah, the same way you been fucking Alana and Sasha while fucking me." I gave him the deuces from behind and walked out the tattoo shop. I knew I was playing a dangerous game, but I was the motherfucking queen of them!

Chapter 2
Draco

It's ten o'clock in the morning on a Saturday and I'm stuck lying here looking at the ceiling, trying to figure out my next move. I couldn't even believe I was up this early on a Saturday morning. Typically I slept until at least twelve or one on the weekend, but sleep hadn't been my friend since I found out Paris was pregnant a week ago. She basically used me for some dick then ghosted my ass like I knew she would. She hadn't answered any of my calls and she had the nerves to change the locks on the doors that I'm paying all the bills for.

I knew a lot of Paris's actions had to do with Jonah. His ass had been up here like he lived out here now. Sasha told me he planned on moving out here but it better not be in the condo I bought for Paris. I didn't have a problem cashing out on her, but I'd be damn if I cashed out on a nigga she fucking. I couldn't blame him for wanting to move out here to be with her though. She got the kind of pussy that if I wasn't married I would have put a ring on her finger just to lock her down.

I'd been trying to think of the best way to approach this situation with Paris. Had she been at home alone I would have been kicked her shit in, but that would raise too many flags with

Jonah. He already suspected that I was having an affair with Paris, but he couldn't prove shit and I didn't need him running his mouth to Sasha. She hadn't mentioned that he had a baby on the way, so that meant either he didn't know yet or he hadn't told her. I'm pretty sure him not saying anything to Sasha about the baby yet had to do a lot with Paris trying to keep it a secret.

Paris trying to hide the pregnancy only proved my point about that being my baby. She claimed it's Jonah's, but I'm not trying to hear that shit. I'd been nutting up in her pussy since day one. If it wasn't for her being on birth control at first she would have been had my kid a while ago. That brought the next question to mind. How the fuck did she get pregnant? I knew she didn't do that shit on purpose. If she wanted to trap a nigga she could have trapped me a long time ago because I was never careful.

Paris and I had discussed her views on kids a while ago and I knew for a fact she didn't want any right now. She just graduated college and was just about to start working toward her career. That was the most important thing to her right now. Her goals in life trumped anything that had to do with a man or starting a family.

I knew any sane married man would be hoping and praying that his side bitch's baby wasn't his, but that's not the case for me. I guess it's funny that I never looked at Paris as my side bitch. Well, that's a lie. When I first met her all I wanted to do was fuck. She was pretty in the face with a nice ass body. When I first laid eyes on her I instantly had visions of her sliding down my pole and her sucking my dick with her beautiful plump lips. I didn't plan on having a full-on affair with her. I was going to fuck then send her about her way, but when I saw that dusty ass diner she was working in I had to help out. Along the way I got to know her better and grew to love her the same way as I loved my wife. I wish I didn't and I'm ashamed to admit it, but it's too late now. I looked at Paris as if she was my girlfriend. I was living the best of both worlds having Paris and Sasha by side.

The thing was, I wanted to be a father more than anything in this world. I'm a rich ass nigga with everything money could buy, so the only thing left for me to do was start my legacy. Sasha didn't want to give me a kid, so who better to give me one than the other woman I loved. I knew if the baby was mine and Sasha found out, she's going to leave my ass. That's just something I'd have to deal with later, though, because I would never abandon my child and I'm damn sure not about to let another nigga raise it as theirs just so my wife's feelings didn't get hurt.

Paris was only a couple months right now, though, so I had some time to figure out how to tell Sasha. My main thing right now was trying to get Paris not to push me away. It would kill me to know I missed out on her pregnancy and Jonah reaped all the benefits. Just thinking about her fucking him while she's possibly pregnant with my baby was enough for me to go to her house and put a bullet in his head right now. It would solve all my problems, but then it would break my wife's heart to find her only sibling in a ditch.

I had to find a way to convince Paris to meet me halfway in this situation. If I had to split appointments with Jonah then I was willing to do that. I couldn't fathom that baby coming out as mine and when he or she grew up, finding out I wasn't there for Paris while she was pregnant. I couldn't take just laying here anymore, so I climbed out of bed and went in the bathroom to take a hot shower. I turned the hot water on and closed my eyes. I stood there for I don't know how long until I felt a set of arms wrap around me.

"Good morning, my love," Sasha spoke.

"Good morning, baby," I replied.

"You couldn't sleep again?" she asked as her hand traveled down to my dick.

"Nope, I tried to lay there for as long as I could without waking you, but I became restless so I decided to shower."

"Are you stressing about something? Maybe if you talk to me about it then I can help. There was a time when we were able to talk about any and everything."

"It's just some shit going on in the streets. With the profession you're in, the less you know the better," I lied, hoping it would stop her from questioning me since we never discussed my street business.

"Okay, well maybe I can help you relieve some of the stress temporarily," she said before dropping to her knees. She placed my dick in her mouth and I tried to push my thoughts to the back of my mind while she topped me off, but right now sex was the last thing on my mind. Flashes of Paris popped up in my head. It was visions of her having the baby smiling with Jonah next to her and even visions of her fucking him. Those thoughts were fucking up my mind and body. It took five minutes for my dick to get hard only for it soften back up.

"What the fuck, Draco? I know whatever's going on with you has to do with more than work because your dick has never gone soft on me before. This some straight bullshit, I'm horny as hell and wanted to fuck. You better get your shit together because if I find out you fucking around on me again, I'm leaving your dog ass," she snapped before getting up and leaving out of the bathroom.

I couldn't even say anything back because she had every right to be mad. Never in my life had my dick gone soft for a bitch let alone my wife. The nights that I fucked Paris for hours I still had stamina to make love to Sasha if she wanted to. This situation was fucking up my marriage already, and I had a feeling this was just the beginning.

I finished my shower then went into the bedroom to start getting dressed. Sasha was sitting on the phone with a scowl on her face. She was talking to somebody about meeting up with them. By the time I was done getting ready she was hanging up the phone.

"Who was that?" I asked.

"Why? It's not like I'm the person on your mind," she replied sarcastically.

"Chill with the bullshit, Sasha. I told you some shit going down in the streets. If it was anything else then I'd talk to you. I'm sorry my shit wouldn't stay hard. If you need to cum that bad I can eat your pussy for you until later on when my head is on straight," I offered, even though I didn't feel like giving head either, but I would if it'd make her feel better.

"Man, I don't want no pity head. I'm good on that. I'll get myself off in the shower."

"That better be where your ass plans on getting off at because you know I'll kill you and whatever nigga you even think about giving my pussy to," I warned her.

"Wow, so you'll kill me for doing the same shit you're doing?" she stated matter of factly.

"What the fuck am I doing, Sasha? I ain't came home smelling like no bitch. Ain't nobody calling me at strange hours. I'm home in bed with your ass every night. What the fuck else do you want from me?"

"This is me you're talking to, Draco. You're just doing a better job at covering up your shit. We both know what's done in the dark always comes to light eventually."

"I'm not trying to hear that shit. If you think I'm fucking around on you still, then why the fuck are you still here with me?"

"Because I love your dumb ass and like I said the first time, I don't have proof, but let's be clear about one thing. If and when I do find out, we'll be having a totally different conversation, Draco. I won't be as forgiving as last time."

"I'm about to go take care of some business. If you need me, call my phone," I said, dismissing the conversation.

"Don't worry, I won't need anything. If I do I'll get it while I'm out with my other nigga," she said with a smirk.

Before she could react, I snatched her ass up by her throat.

"What the fuck did you just say to me? You know not to fucking play with me like this. I'll kill your ass right here, right now, Sasha."

"Stop Draco, you're hurting me," she said with tears falling from her eyes.

I loosened my grip but I didn't completely let her go.

"Who the fuck are you about to meet up with?"

"You know I was only joking. I'm not going to fuck anybody else. I respect the vows we shared. Jonah is on his way over here to pick me up. He wants me to go look at some houses with him. I was only playing. I'm not about to go see no nigga. Apparently he and Paris are more serious than I thought because he plans on asking her to move in with him."

I tried my best to keep my same facial expression because if I showed how I was really feeling it would give me and Paris away. So instead of walking away like I should have, I took my anger out on my wife.

"Give me your fucking phone," I demanded.

"What? Are you serious?" she asked, surprised.

"You damn right I am because you let that slick shit come out of your mouth twice."

Sasha walked away from me and grabbed her phone from the nightstand. She threw it at me then stormed off into the bathroom.

I unlocked her phone with my facial recognition. I looked through her call log and the last call was from Jonah. I was tempted to go through her text messages but if she was anything like me, I'm not going to find anything. I tossed her phone on the bed then grabbed my keys and left the room. I hopped in my car then drove around for about thirty minutes to kill time before heading in the direction of Paris's condo. I drove around the block a few times to make sure that Jonah was gone for good before parking.

I headed in the building and went upstairs to her floor. I knocked twice and Paris opened the door without even saying who is it.

"Draco, what are you doing here? I thought Jonah had forgotten something."

"Nah, he's gone, I made sure that he was out of the area before I parked," I told her as I moved her out of the way because clearly, she wasn't about to let me in.

"Okay, that's still not explaining why you're here," she said.

My eyes traveled across her body. She was only wearing a white half shirt with a pair of black bikini panties. I could see her nipples through the shirt so it was obvious she wasn't wearing a bra. All the blood in my body rushed to my dick, making it brick up. Clearly there wasn't anything wrong with my manhood. Here it was my wife was giving me head and I couldn't stay hard while Paris hadn't even touched me and I was ready to dick her down. I pushed those thoughts to the back of my mind, though, because that wasn't the reason I was here.

"I came to talk, Paris. You come to my office and you tell me that you're pregnant by Jonah then disappear."

"I didn't think there was anything else for us to talk about. I thought you would be done with me since I'm pregnant by your brother-in-law."

"How the fuck do you know that's his baby? You were

fucking both of us so it's only right that I have a right to be updated."

"How exactly do you plan on that working?"

"I can alternate appointments with him. I want to be here up until the baby is born. When we get the DNA test done if it comes back negative, you have my word. I'll leave you alone and respect your relationship with him, but if that's my baby there's no way in hell you will ever get rid of me."

"Okay, say I agree to this, what if the baby comes out as yours, then what, Draco? You're married to my boyfriend's sister. I'm willing to keep my mouth shut and allow Jonah to think it's his baby. Our secret can continue to stay between us."

"You done lost your fucking mind if you think I'll let Jonah raise my child as his. If that's my baby, he or she will be named after me. I'll deal with the consequences of Sasha when the time comes. She's never been your problem before and she won't be now," I advised her before sitting down on her couch. She looked like she wanted to protest but instead, she sighed and sat on the couch next to me so we could finish our conversation.

Chapter 3
Sasha

Draco thought he was fucking slick. I gave him my phone so he could go through it. I knew he would check the call log because he thought he knew me. I had Jhayce's number under his number so he wouldn't know a fucking thing. I knew Draco was fucking over me, but I didn't have solid proof or know who the bitch was. Just like he had shit on his mind, so did I. Jhayce was giving me everything that Draco gave me when we first got married. Late-night conversations, falling asleep on the phone. On one of those nights, I muted the call because Draco came in the house drunk out his fucking mind wanting some pussy. Of course, I couldn't deny my husband. I rode his dick with Jhayce on mute. Draco never paid attention. That's how I knew he was cheating. My shit was too easy. Men would tell on themselves when cheating, but women never got caught.

Soon as I heard him backing out the driveway, I ran in the bathroom so I could get dressed. All I wanted was some dick and Draco was on some other shit. I wanted to try and ease it but clearly his dick had other plans because it wouldn't get hard for me. Either he'd just fucked a bitch when he came in a few hours ago or the bitch had him in the doghouse. That raised a million fucking red flags but I couldn't trip because I was doing my own dirt, just better.

As I slipped on my trench coat, I stood in front of my full-length mirror. Draco had to be a stupid motherfucker to cheat on me. My hourglass figure hugged the blue lace teddy and garter belt getup that I put on. Just as I put my left arm in the coat, my phone buzzed. I picked it up and it was Jonah calling. Shit, I forgot he wanted to go look at homes for him and Paris to move into. I'd already contacted a realtor but he was adamant on me coming with him to look at the homes.

"What's up, brother?" I asked him.

"Why you sound breathless, and you must've forgot about me because you didn't call me back with a location." I didn't like his tone but I let it slide because I knew he was mentally fucked up.

What a lot of people didn't know was that Jonah suffered from bipolar depression. It started when my father put too much pressure on him about his profession. My father was the type of man that got a hard-on for perfection. My mother was submissive so what he said went, no questions asked. Jonah even tried to commit suicide because the last woman he invested his everything into fucked him over with his best friend. As of today, they were married with kids like my brother was never with the bitch. That triggered something in him, and he hadn't been right ever since. I hoped that Paris's intentions were pure and genuine because I didn't need him sinking into a deep depression if her young ass decided to break his heart. I won't go into detail because I'd already given too much away. Jonah had his own story to tell.

"I didn't forget but I did have a prior engagement to attend to before I came with you," I told him calmly because I didn't want to set him off.

"You know how important this is to me, Sasha. I want everything to be perfect for her because she deserves it, but I want your approval first," he huffed in the phone like he was frustrated. I looked down at my attire and knew I couldn't go with him dressed like this. Plus, I had Jhayce waiting. I didn't want to cancel on Jonah but the dick was calling me. I guess I was taking too long to answer him because he spoke before I could get a word out.

"Let's just do the shit tomorrow because clearly you had other plans and forgot about me," he gritted, and I knew he was pissed. True enough, I did forget about our plans but was glad that he chose to reschedule.

"I love you Jonah, and I'll make it up to you. I'll take you to Baskin Robbins and get your favorite." I put on my best sad voice because I knew he would fall for it. He had a sweet tooth for a large banana split with extra whip cream and fudge.

"You know just what to say to get a nigga right." I could hear the smile in his voice.

"No, just my brother. I love you Jonah, and I got you tomorrow," I told him, and he told me back before we ended the call. I'm glad I dodged that bullet because I was feigning for Jhayce like a dog in heat.

I sat at my vanity table to apply minimal makeup. A little concealer with blue eyeshadow and lips gloss. I reached for my heels and slid my feet in them one by one. I stood and grabbed my clutch, keys, and purse when I heard a door open and close. My hand started to shake because if Draco came back and saw me dressed like this, I knew he would beat my ass. Granted, he never put his hands on me but when a nigga was mad enough, he would go upside ya head. I heard the footsteps coming up the stairs. I panicked. My purse and everything I was holding dropped to the floor in a thud. I knew I was caught. There was no explanation for me walking out the house as a married woman dressed like a fucking stripper. My heart palpitated out my chest as my palms began to sweat because I didn't know what to do. My head went from left to right trying to figure out if I should take my clothes off and hide them and try to put something more decent on, but I didn't have time to. I heard the steps getting closer and closer. It would have been stupid for me to hide in the closet. The door creaked open as I prepared for the best lie to leave my lips.

"What the fuck are you doing here? How do you know where I live, Jhayce?" I shrieked, looking around like Draco was here.

"You were taking too long, bae, and you never turn your location off on your phone," he told me, and I was scared. This entire situation was creeping me out and turning me on at the same time.

"I ran into a little bump and was running a little late, but that doesn't mean you can pop up at my house. What if my husband was here?" I told him as he walked closer into the room, closing and locking the door.

"I saw that nigga leave and went with my move." He pulled the lapel on my coat. "You wore this for me?" he asked with lust in his eyes, and I knew I was in trouble. I couldn't fuck this nigga in the same house I shared with my husband but from the way he looked at me, those plans were about to change and fast.

"What are you doing, Jhayce?! You cannot be here! What if my husband comes back?" I rocked from left to right. This nigga was freaking me out by the minute, and I didn't like it. I felt violated.

"You been watching me?" I asked him, giving attitude.

"Hell no, I'm not some creep. You were just taking too long and I got tired of waiting. We missed the reservations anyway," he said like he didn't see shit wrong with him popping up at my damn house. He had better get the hell out and quick. He walked closer to me, slowly pulling the jacket from my body. I felt my body shiver with anticipation of what was to come. I knew I was walking in dangerous territory, but I didn't give a fuck. I was living in the moment. I knew whatever happened after this this day would change my mind frame forever. Draco was a lot of things, but I knew he would never fuck a bitch in the house that we shared let alone the fucking bed.

Jhayce grabbed my waist, backing me up to the bed. My pussy got moist as he sat me down and opened my legs wide. His hand ran from my heels to my waist as he slid my panties down to my ankles, pulling them off. He licked his lips and I knew all bets were off. He took off his suit jacket, throwing it on the bed. I leaned back on my elbows and watched him as he kneeled before me like he was about to praise the pussy. A light bulb went off in my head and I tried to close my thighs. I couldn't disrespect my husband like that. The guilt started to set in and we hadn't even fucked or sucked yet.

"Just let me taste her and then we can leave." He slowly pushed my thighs back open with his massive hands. His fingers grazed my clit and my head fell back. All common sense went out the window. My soul was filled with lust as his middle finger penetrated me and his thumb circled my clit.

"Mmmmmm," was all that left my throat as his entire face engulfed my pussy. I felt his beard brush my asshole and I squirted all over his face.

"Damn, this pussy taste good and it's all mine." My eyes popped open at the sound of his words, and reality sat in about what the fuck we were doing. I sat up as he stood up. He was unbuckling his pants and my mouth watered.

"Wait, we can't do this here, Jhayce. I will not disrespect my husband like this," I told him, never breaking eye contact with his dick. He'd pulled it out and started to massage it. I was stuck between a hard rod and my wet pussy. I wanted to hop on his dick but not at my house.

"Man, fuck that nigga. I just ate yo' pussy on the same bed y'all fucking sleep in and you trying to tell me I can't fuck you on it? Man, bust this pussy open and let Daddy in." He stared at me hard and my legs opened involuntarily. I couldn't control my body. He had complete control. He climbed between my legs, pushing me further into the bed. He kissed my neck, biting and sucking leaving marks, but I didn't care because that shit had my pussy on fire. My clit pulsated as I felt his head at my opening. With one stroke he was completely inside of me, making my back arch from the bed. His hands palmed my ass cheeks to control the rhythm. His strokes were slow and precise, and his dick moved in and out of me.

"I ain't never leaving this pussy alone. That nigga gotta share this." His strokes became faster and I moaned louder. I'd never witnessed this side of Jhayce before and it was making my pussy wetter. This the type of shit I wanted from Draco, but he always wanted to handle me like I was so fragile. I wanted Draco to be in control in the bedroom, but he didn't. The shit Jhayce was saying scared me because clearly he wasn't letting the pussy go.

"I'm 'bout to nut Sash, where you want it at?" he moaned, looking at me.

"You know where I want it at, Daddy," I told him. I knew he couldn't nut in me and definitely not on my sheets. He pulled out of me as nut dripped from his tip and skeeted in my face. I drank that shit up like it was ice-cold milk. After he emptied his seed all over my face and mouth, I sat up and looked at him. I felt dirty. Not because his nut was in my face but because I had just committed the ultimate betrayal. I tried to grab my coat, but Jhayce yanked it from me.

"It's too late to worry about covering up and feeling guilty now. What's done is done and I don't regret shit about it. You took too long to come to me so I took a chance coming to you. Go shower and shit so we can actually go on our date. The sex is out the way for now." He winked at me, pulling me to my feet. I went to the bathroom to get in the shower.

As the hot water ran down my body, the tears ran down my face. I had fucked up and didn't know how to face Draco knowing what I'd done. I'd made accusations of him cheating but I was actually doing the shit and in our bed that we shared. I was scum, but the sex was good. I had no one to blame but me because I let this shit get out of control. I shouldn't have given in to Jhayce's advances, but he was sexy as fuck, and I couldn't help it. I used my loofa to try and scrub the dirt from my body, but it was more mental than physical. I felt like shit. I hurriedly washed the rest of my body and hopped out the shower to get dressed.

I walked out the bathroom with my plush towel wrapped around my body. I noticed Jhayce sitting on the chair going through his phone. I moved around the room trying to fix shit the way it was before I walked in my closet to find something to put on. After grabbing a bra and panty set and a sundress with a pair of sandals, I walked out the closet and put my stuff on the bed. I grabbed my vanilla body butter and started to lather my body before slipping on my clothes. He was eerily quiet as he looked at his phone like he was studying it. I sat on the bed to put my sandals on and the quietness was killing me.

"What are you staring at your phone so hard for, Jhayce?" I didn't mean to have an attitude but his facial expressions were making me suspicious. He stood up and walked over to me fully dressed like we hadn't just finished fucking. I stood as he approached me. I looked at him funny until he turned his phone around with the screen facing me. I looked at the screen and there was a video of us having sex. It started when he first walked in the door and didn't end until I got up and went into the bathroom. Then he took his camera and waved it around the room, videoing my entire bedroom. I was flabbergasted. I felt the tears forming in my eyes. He was trying to blackmail me. I tried to snatch the phone from him but he backed up just in time.

"What the fuck are you doing, Jhayce?! Why the fuck would you video us having sex in my bedroom?" I yelled at him. I swung my arm to smack his face, but he stopped it midair.

"Don't you ever try to put yo' fucking hands on me, Sasha. I might not be a thug ass nigga like yo' husband, but I had a life before this shit here. No, it's not blackmail, just a little collateral just in case you try to take the pussy from me. How would Draco feel if he saw this video of his perfect wife fucking another nigga in the bed that both of you sleep in every night?" He paused, then his index finger tapped his temple. "Or if I put this shit on every social media platform and tag you in it and sabotage your entire career? I could do even better and turn this shit into HR and ruin you. I don't give a fuck about the job because my firm is in London. I got something to fall back on, but do you?" he asked, and I couldn't answer.

My body was in a state of shock. My entire body trembled because he had my entire life in the palm of his hands and there was nothing I could do about it. I was crushed. I thought I could trust him, but now I knew I couldn't. I walked closer to him in his personal space with my poker face on. I wanted to cry, kick, and scream or even punch him in the mouth because of the smirk that was plastered on his face. He thought he had one up on me, but I had a surprise for his ass. I took the tip of my nail to his chin and slightly lifted it.

"If you think about showing this video to my husband or anybody for that matter, he will decapitate your fucking body and send it to your mother. If he leaves me, so what. It ain't hard to get another nigga. I got you, didn't I? Don't fuck with me, Jhayce, or he will end you, and that's on God himself. Now, are you ready for lunch?" I asked him, grabbing my shit and walking out the door with him not too far behind me. Checkmate.

Chapter 4
Draco

The conversation between me and Paris went better than I thought. I just knew she was going to try to stick to that bullshit about Jonah being the daddy. Deep down I knew she knew that's my seed she's carrying. She's just trying to go the easy route because being with Jonah was less complicated. I knew I told her I'd respect her relationship if the baby wasn't mine, and I meant that shit. It's time for me to do right by my wife. However, if the baby was mine she might as well end things with Jonah because I would permanently be in her and my child's life with no questions asked.

Paris and I discussed how things were going with the pregnancy. She also told me she knew for a while and had no intentions on telling me. Once she started showing she was going to just stop working at the shop for good. She was actually going to up and move and act like what we had never happened. I was tripping on how she thought I was never going to find out about the baby. Being that she's with my wife's brother, she had to know Jonah would eventually tell Sasha and she'd tell me. I was curious about what she was going to do when we went to visit them to see the mystery baby. She said she hadn't thought that far ahead and that was obvious. Even though Alana was on some shady shit, she had done me a favor. Speaking of her, it was time for me to cut her ass off. I wasn't worried about her telling Sasha about Paris because then she knew I'd never speak to her again, and that would hurt her worse.

I tried my luck with fucking Paris before I left her house. She was acting like she didn't want to break a nigga off but eventually she cracked. My head was buried between her thighs when Jonah called her phone. She stopped me from taking care of business to take his call. I was pissed because he had only been gone for about forty minutes so I didn't understand why he was calling her already. When she finished the call she hurriedly got dressed and told me I had to go because Jonah was on his way back. Something about Sasha being busy so they had to reschedule. That was news to me, but I figured she probably told him that because she was upset with me, so I shrugged it off and left.

I wasn't in the mood to argue with Sasha and I wanted to make things right. Paris had me horny and since I couldn't fuck her that meant I needed to go home and fuck my wife, and the only way that was going to happen was if I kissed up to her. I went to Pandora and grabbed a couple charms for her bracelet because she wasn't into fancy jewelry. After that I grabbed some roses then last but not least, I ordered us some food from STK Steakhouse to go.

I drove home and parked in the garage next to Sasha's car. I entered the house and set up our food on the table along with her gifts. The downstairs area was quiet but that wasn't unusual since Sasha spent the weekends in front of our bedroom TV. I walked up the stairs and into our empty bedroom. The stench of cologne instantly hit my nostrils causing my nostrils to flare because it wasn't the scent of my cologne. That made me get into straight detective mode because Sasha talked a lot of shit, but I knew she ain't have a nigga in my house. I'd always done my dirt, but I never disrespected my wife to the point where I brought them to the house we shared.

I took a deep breath as I walked further into our bedroom. My eyes fell on the blue lace thong that was on the floor next to the bed. Sasha didn't have those on before I left and they weren't on the floor. Also, our bed wasn't made and that was something Sasha's ass always did. I walked closer to the bed and there was a big ass wet spot on our red sheets. I couldn't help but chuckle because she didn't even have the decency to change the sheets. She was sloppy as hell with this shit, so I knew this was something new for her. If she knew what was good for her and whoever she was fucking, she would have thought this through better.

I sat down on the chaise and dialed Sasha's number. I wanted to see if she was as slick as she thought she was.

"Hey baby," she answered.

"Hey, how's the house shopping with Jonah going?" I asked, already knowing the answer.

"It's going slow as hell. We've been to three houses and he still hasn't found anything he likes. This is going to take a lot longer than I thought. About what time do you think you're going to be home?" she asked me while lying through her teeth.

"I'm not sure. Some shit came up that I have to handle, so it won't be until sometime this evening. I was just calling to apologize about earlier. We can discuss it tonight when we're both at home though."

"Okay, you really don't have to apologize though. It was my fault for how things turned out," she said.

That right there showed me that she was guilty as hell. She would never concede before me because what happened earlier was in fact my fault and not hers.

"Alright, I'll talk to you later. I love you," I told her for what might be the last time.

"I love you too," she replied, not skipping a beat.

I hung up the phone and went to Find My iPhone app. I never went to this but Sasha just pushed me to the limit. It wasn't even about her cheating because God knew with all the dirt I did I deserved this shit, but it's the fact that she let a nigga come up in our crib. With the lifestyle I lived, no one should know where we lived if they weren't close to us. Hell, Paris didn't even know where I lived. She never asked and I never volunteered because we always went to her crib or a hotel.

I looked at Sasha's location and it was showing a Motel 6 by the airport. I immediately saw red because they weren't even trying to be discreet about the shit. Here I was only going to hotels out of state and they were right here in town. She was basically saying fuck me, and I'd killed niggas for less. I couldn't even believe Sasha would let a nigga fuck her in a Motel 6. This was how I knew she was working off emotion, because she didn't settle for shit like this.

I walked out of the room and back out of the house. Hopping in my car, I drove straight to the trap house so I could grab one of the burner cars. I didn't give a fuck that it was broad daylight. Somebody was about to get some of this hot lead in their ass. I didn't want to tell anyone what I was about to do because they would try to talk me out of it.

I drove to the motel and sat outside in my car to scope the area. I didn't know what car they came in so I had no idea which room could be theirs. The only thing I could do now was wait. I didn't give a fuck how long it took, I wasn't going anywhere until I let off a couple rounds. I knew what I was doing was stupid, but I didn't give a fuck. I warned Sasha not to play with me. I didn't know why she was acting like she didn't know who she was married to.

Two hours went by when I finally saw her walking out of the motel room hanging on to this fake Dave East want-to-be looking ass nigga. He was saying something that made her smile from ear to ear. From the outside looking in, you would think they were the perfect couple. The bitch still had her rock on her finger, adding more soil to our marriage. I couldn't remember the last time Sasha smiled like that with me. I felt like shit because I drove my wife to step out on our marriage. If I was a better man, I would have discreetly driven away and talked about this with my wife when she got home, but we all know I'm not shit and that would be going against the grain.

I waited for them to climb in his black Bentley and pull off before pulling off behind them. I stayed two cars behind them trying to think of the perfect spot to jump into action because I didn't want to do it by my house. As if on cue, he pulled into a Circle K gas station and that was perfect timing. It almost felt like this was meant to happen. I drove up on the side of his car and emptied my clip in it before he or Sasha could react. I hurried up and drove away from the gas station and back to the warehouse. I dialed Paris's number and drove in the direction of one of my old spots. It took me twenty minutes to finally get her to agree to meet up with me.

I walked in the house and went straight to the bathroom to shower. I didn't have any blood on me but it's part of my routine to get rid of the evidence. I scratched the serial number off my gun and put it away so I could dispose of it later. I didn't know the injuries of the guy that was with Sasha because most of the bullets hit him. I made sure to only shoot Sasha in her arm. As much as I was pissed off with her, I didn't have it in me to kill my own wife. I already knew the shooting was going to be on the news because she was a prestigious judge.

I made my way down the stairs and straight to my bar. I opened a bottle of Henny and knocked back shot after shot. I lost track of how many shots I had by the time the sound of my doorbell went off. I got up from the bar stool and staggered over to the door, letting Paris in.

As soon as she stepped foot in the house, I pulled her close to me, inhaling her scent.

"Draco, are you okay?" Paris asked, concerned.

"No, I need you right now, Paris," I told her as I lifted her dress over her ass.

She looked like she wanted to object, but I didn't give her a chance before sliding her underwear to the side and burying myself inside of her. I stood her up against the wall and fucked her until her body started trembling and she was coming all over my dick, and I was right behind her.

I held Paris while we caught our breath before letting her down. She didn't say anything as she walked away and headed to the bathroom across the hall. I sat on the couch for about fifteen minutes until she finally came out and sat next to me.

"What's going on with you, Draco?" Paris finally asked.

"After I left your house I went to make a couple runs before heading home. Sasha was mad at me, so I went to make up with her. When I got to the house she wasn't there, but it smelled like some nigga's cologne and there was a big ass wet spot in my bed. She basically fucked someone else in our bed. I pulled up her location and went to the motel they were at and shot up his car."

"Draco, are you serious? You just finished fucking me but shot at your wife because she was with another man?"

"I shot at her ass because she fucked him in our house. I would have definitely still fucked the nigga up, but I would have eventually let her slide."

"Are they okay?"

"Not sure, I'll know something once she calls me. She'll

most likely wait to call me though because then she'll have to explain what she was doing in the car with another man."

"That's fucked up on so many levels, Draco. You could have killed your damn wife."

"I know that she's not dead. I know how to aim, I only hit her in the arm."

Just as those words left my mouth, Paris's phone started to ring. It was Jonah calling to let her know that he had to rush to the hospital because Sasha had been shot. Paris agreed to meet him at the hospital, and the hospital was calling me shortly after that. I allowed Paris to leave in order to give her a head start so that we weren't showing up together. I needed time to clear my head before going to the hospital. I was going to have to play the distraught husband role. I couldn't wait to see Sasha's explanation to this shit. I was going to tell her I found out about her and the man as soon as she stepped foot back in our house.

Chapter 5
Sasha

What the fuck just happened?! I thought to myself as I dialed the police. Someone had shot up the car that Jhayce and I were in. I looked over at Jhayce and he was barely moving. This shit was all my fault. I shouldn't have been cheating on my husband and fucking my side nigga in my house. Once the ambulance arrived, they took me in the back. I had four gunshots in the arm looking like a fucking domino effect. Who the fuck would shoot at us? What the fuck was Jhayce really into? I watched as they pulled Jhayce from the car and put him on a gurney. They rushed him to the helicopter because he had to be airlifted to the hospital. That wasn't a good sign. I knew from watching TV shows that when a person was airlifted, they were damn near dead. They wrapped my arm with gauze to stop the bleeding, but I couldn't feel that shit because my adrenaline had yet to be brought down.

Once we got to the hospital I was immediately brought to surgery. They removed the bullets, and thank God I didn't lose my arm. They brought me to recovery, and I noticed Jonah sitting in the chair by the window asleep.

"Jonah," I called his name, and his eyes opened and he yawned, stretching his arms to the sky. Paris was sitting on his lap with her head in the crook of his neck asleep. They were so cute together. I loved Paris for my brother because she seemed to keep him levelheaded. I knew Jonah would be pissed because I'd put him in the middle of my shit, and I had to think of something quick to tell him because I had to have an explanation as to why and how I got shot. I knew Draco wouldn't go for me getting shot while looking for a fucking house.

"What the fuck, Sasha?! The fuck were you doing to get shot and you had to reschedule helping me look for a house with me and Paris," he gritted, and I knew he was pissed because his eyes were red and spit spewed from his mouth. Paris wasn't supposed to know about the house, but the cat was out the bag now. Paris shifted a little but kept her position on his lap and continued to sleep. She slept hard as hell. His voice carried and his baritone was deep, but I guess she was just that tired. I needed him calm so he was levelheaded when shit went down.

"First of all, did you contact Draco?" I was hoping that he didn't because I didn't need him coming up here clowning.

"Nah, I ain't call that nigga, but I'm sure the doctor or police officers did because yo' ass was shot, but who the fuck was the nigga in the car with you? I heard the officer say you were on the passenger side, so who the fuck were you with, and don't lie?" he barked at me like he was my husband. I thought about Jhayce and prayed that he was okay.

"Oh my God, is he okay? Where did they bring him?" I asked quietly because I didn't want Jonah to keep raising his voice. His deep ass voice would draw every fucking nurse into this room and I didn't need that.

"The nigga in ICU barely breathing from what the doctors are saying. He was shot everywhere but under his fucking feet, but I find the shit strange that he's clinging to fucking life and you only got shot in the arm," he said, cocking his head to the side, "So what the fuck is really going on? Somebody behind that nigga?" he asked as I tried to sit up in the bed with his assistance. I hadn't really thought about somebody possibly being behind him, but then I thought about the shit he was telling me back at my house.

"No, we work together, and before you ask the obvious, yes, I am fucking him. Don't judge me because you wouldn't understand. All I need you to do is say that we went to the store and when you got out, there was a drive-by that I was caught in while you went to pay for the gas," I explained to him, and his brows wrinkled. He started to laugh.

"Draco is a street nigga. You really think he gon' believe that shit? I wouldn't even believe it if it was true. You not convincing at all, Sasha." He had a scowl on his face but I kept a stoned face. I didn't know what else to say when Draco came in here asking for an explanation. I had to make it believable. Paris stood and rubbed his back, trying to soothe the raging bull that was trying to expose itself. I noticed Paris looking at me with a look in her eyes that I couldn't quite process, but I didn't like it and would address it with Draco later.

"Well, what the fuck do you think I should tell him, Sherlock?" I asked him, irritated by his laughter. This was a life or death situation and I had no clue what I was going to do.

"Did you bring my clothes like I asked?" I asked, and he stopped laughing. He got up and went to the counter to get my duffle bag. I yanked it from him to open it and pull out my toiletries and clothes. My arm was in a sling with a cast. I got up and walked to the bathroom, closing the door behind me. I tried my best to clean myself and get dressed, and it took a little longer than I intended it to. I was hoping that I could hurry, get dressed and discharged before Draco could even get here because I didn't feel like hearing his mouth. I put on my joggers and shirt and slipped my feet into my slippers when I heard a loud bang, like a door opening and slamming shut. I was almost scared to open the door thinking it was Draco. I grabbed the knob and went to turn it but stopped when I heard a female's voice

"Where that bitch at?! I know she in here! The hoe been fucking my husband like I wouldn't find out! I had my private investigator following his bitch ass for months. I know he cheating with that street hood ass bitch and that's why the fuck he got shot fucking with her!" My hands trembled but I didn't open the door. I knew this motherfucker didn't have a fucking wife and was trying to blackmail me. I didn't need this drama right now.

"Hold up, slow down, what are you talking about ma'am?" I heard Jonah's voice trying to calm the lady down.

"You know exactly what the fuck I'm talking about. You trying to spare this bitch when my husband is fighting for his life because he decided to deal with a hood rat bitch!" I heard her say.

"Hold up, don't come in here with all that rah-rah shit when you don't even know who the fucking patient is," I heard Paris's voice say and smiled. She was defending me and I respected her for that. "And she ain't no hoodrat bitch so stop playing, because I know you did your homework already. Get the fuck outta here," Paris continued her rant, but I could hear Jonah mumble something and she calmed down. There I was sitting in the bathroom listening to the wife of the nigga I was cheating on my husband with argue with my family when it should have been me out there defending myself because I created all this shit. I wasn't a hoodrat and his fucking wife knew that. The bitch was just mad. I slowly creaked the door open and everybody got silent. I noticed Jonah holding Paris around the waist and the mystery woman standing behind the closed door. Our eyes met and I thought she was about to rush me. Paris must have thought the same thing because she broke away from Jonah and came toward me.

"Bitch, you the reason my husband dying and you walked away with just a fucked-up arm!" she yelled and looked closer to my face. "Hold up, aren't you the criminal fucking judge in the building that he works in?" She looked at me and I looked at Paris like she would help me. She didn't know me that well but I did appreciate her for stepping in.

"Yes, and so what? This lady not fucking your husband because she got her own." Paris twirled her neck, walking up to the bitch's face. She was defending like I was her bestie or some shit.

"Nah Paris, this ain't yo' battle to fight, I got this," I told her and slightly moved her to the side. I walked up to her, putting my finger to her head.

"Yes, bitch, I'm fucking yo' husband because clearly yo' pussy ain't working right," I told her and continued, "I don't regret it and this shit wouldn't have happened tonight but we were about to go for round two." I broke that bitch's heart with my words because it displayed on her face. She was shocked. All that fucking yelling and bucking she was doing before she actually stopped. I could tell Jhayce liked a certain type of woman. It's crazy because his wife and I had the same style and dress down to the hairstyles. I was a little rusty because of the clothes Jonah picked out for me, but I didn't care because I knew I was that bitch.

"And for the record, I'm far from a hoodrat bitch. I'm sure you did your research so this shit ain't have nothing to do with me. If you have your private investigators watching everything, then you would know I had nothing to do with it," I told her, and she rolled her eyes to the ceiling.

"Listen, you little judge bitch, I tracked everything in Jhayce's phone so I knew he was at your fucking house. I will bring his phone to the Human Resources Department and ruin your career, bitch. I have access to everything," she spewed in my face, and my heart dropped. I had to get to that phone before she did because I couldn't afford for my job to see that video.

"If that's what you feel like you have to do, have at it, but remember, it's your husband's phone and he is on it as well, so feel free to show text messages and phones calls," I told her, leaving out the video because I knew she hadn't seen it. Nine times outta ten, the hospital had his phone and hadn't given it to her yet.

"You a bold bitch to fuck my husband like you aren't already married," she said, looking at my wedding rings that were on my left hand.

"It's time for you to go," I told her because my heart told me that Draco would walk in art any moment and I didn't need this wanna be Barbie bitch airing my dirty laundry in front of my husband.

"You right, bitch, I'm leaving to go check on MY husband and I suggest you do the fucking same." She tossed her hair over her shoulder before walking out the room.

"Yo, watch where the fuck you going," I heard Draco bark as he pushed past the bitch and walked in the door. His eyes went to Paris and Jonah before they made their way to me. The look in his eyes was of hate and a little bit of hurt. The hate outweighed the hurt ten times over. He rolled his eyes at Jonah and came to me.

"How the fuck you get shot looking at houses with your brother, Sasha?" he asked as calmly as he could while helping me put on my jacket.

"Can we discuss this in the privacy of our home please,

Draco?" I asked, nodding my head toward Jonah and Paris. Draco held a smirk on his face.

"You sure you wanna do that?" I saw the fire dancing in his eyes. I nodded my head and answered.

"Yeah, I'm just waiting on my discharge papers." I tried to kiss his lips but he dodged it. I guess he was upset because I'd put myself in harm's way.

Draco

I played the prodigal husband very well. I heard the entire conversation the bitch had with my wife about her husband. I knew what the fuck I'd done and didn't regret it because I knew Sasha was playing with me. The disrespectful bitch had the nigga in my house, it's the principle of the situation. The way Jonah stood behind Paris with his hands caressing her belly made me wanna air this bitch out, but I held my cool because I didn't want to make shit worse between us. I walked over to Sasha to help her finish getting dressed before she was discharged. My mind was still fucked up because here I was standing in the middle of my side bitch and my wife. My anger got the best of me as I turned to Jonah and Paris.

"Y'all can go, I got her from here." I looked at both of them and couldn't miss the sad look on Paris's face. I knew that face all too well because when she couldn't get her way with me, she would make that face and I would give in.

"Are you sure, because that—" Before Paris could finish her sentence, Jonah hopped in the fucking conversation.

"Yeah, we 'bout to head out now that you're here so I can lay Paris down for the night," he said with a smirk on his face like he knew some shit I didn't know about. But little did his pea-brain ass know, I knew everything including that the baby Paris was carrying was mine. Paris was hesitant to take a step, looking at me to save her, but I wouldn't. It wasn't that I didn't want to, but she'd made her decision and now she had to stick to it. She chose that nigga over me and that's some shit I had to deal with on my own. As of now, I had some shit to say to my wife that I didn't need them to hear, so it was in their best interest that they leave.

"We can all meet back at the house," Sasha said, and I gave her a look. She was scared. Scared of what I might do to her ass, but she just didn't know I wasn't going to do her ass anything.

"Nah, I'm tired and this lil' baby is kicking my ass so it's time for me to eat and sleep," Paris said with her eyes trained on mine as she rubbed her belly. She was really fucking with me and putting her life in danger. She smiled like I didn't just have my entire face in her pussy. I'd let her have that, but this ain't the last she would see me. I gave a half smile to Paris as I dapped Jonah up. I waited until they were out the door and probably halfway down the hallway before I went in on this bitch. I calmly sat my keys on the bed and cracked my knuckles and neck. If I had a fucking camera I would have snapped the expression of her face because she was scared shitless. I always told my wife that I left my street life in the fucking streets, but she decided to cross me and bring the streets into my fucking home and in my bed.

"Before you answer my fucking questions, I want you to think about the fucking stories you heard about me in the streets," I told her and walked closer, turning her to face me. She yelped in pain, but I didn't give a fuck about all that because I was the nigga behind it.

"Where the fuck did you go after I left you at the house?" I stood before her rocking from side to side. She looked at me and I knew she was about to use one of her antics from the court-room, but that shit wasn't gon' work because I was the judge in the fucking streets. She leaned on one side and chuckled, pissing me off a little further.

"Me and Jonah had finished viewing a house and he needed to stop for gas." She stumbled over her words so I knew she was lying. "I told him that it was a bad neighborhood but he insisted on needing gas before the car ran out," she said and started to squeeze tears out her eyes, but that shit didn't move me. I knew everything. That's why I told Jonah to leave. If he would have lied for his sister, I would have snapped his fucking neck. I was about to grab her neck but the doctor and nurse walking in saved this dumb bitch.

"Okay Sasha, here is your discharge paperwork and instructions. Check with orthopedics in about six weeks for that cast," he said, and he and the nurse left quietly. Soon as the door closed, I was on her. My hand wrapped around her neck as I lifted her from the ground.

"Bitch, you wasn't with Jonah, you was with that nigga that's dying upstairs," I told her and dragged her toward the door. Her nails scratched at my hands drawing blood, but I could take that shit. I dragged her to the stairs and up to the fourth floor. We got in front of the door where the nigga was laying. It's amazing what a few bands could do with the right nurse. Money really was the root of all evil. I peeked in the room and noticed the same lady, which was his wife, leaning over checking the machines and making sure he was comfortable. She turned and we hid behind the wall. I peeked as she walked toward the door and slipped out as we slipped in. We walked close to his bed and I pushed her neck toward the nigga's face.

"Does this look like fucking Jonah? Better yet, is this the fucking realtor?" I asked, pushing her head closer and closer to him.

"Stop this Draco, please," she begged, but I wasn't trying to hear that shit.

"He ain't neither one because I remember seeing this nigga when I surprised you for lunch one afternoon, remember?" I asked her. "That nigga gave me a look like I killed his best fucking friend. I didn't understand that shit then, but I do now. It's yo' fucking fault this young man is in this condition because you couldn't keep yo' fucking legs closed," I told her, applying more pressure to her neck. I was already out my fucking mind because Paris walked out with that nigga Jonah, and her fucking a nigga that she worked with in my house was icing on the fucking cake.

"You fucking this nigga, huh?" I gritted in her ear, and she tried to nod her head. "Nah, don't answer that, because that lady loves her husband and I wouldn't inflict that type of pain on her and pull all these fucking machines apart and kill him, but this ain't on him, this all you." I yanked her head back and let her go. I straightened up my clothes and yanked her discharge papers out her hand. Her eyes cried real tears, eyes bloodshot and everything. Bitch had a little snot running out her nose, but it didn't move me.

"You better beat me to the fucking car," I told her as I ripped the paperwork the doctor gave me, including her prescriptions for her pain meds.

"Draco, I need that paperwork, that was my pain medication." She winced before rolling her eyes at me.

"Bitch, what's about to happen to you, Percocet, Vicodin and not even a fucking Lortab will help you. Get the fuck to the car," I yelled at her, and she beat her fucking feet to the elevator. I turned around and looked at the nigga laying in the bed with tubes coming from every part of his body. I looked at the socket on the wall. My first mind was to pull the fucking plug and end his ass, but I wanted him to suffer. Plus, his wife didn't do shit wrong but marry the wrong nigga.

"I'm sorry, do you know my husband?" Her voice was sweet and innocent. Nothing like the voice I'd heard when I was standing outside Sasha's room. "Oh, I remember you from the other room. What are you doing in here?" she asked me before walking toward her husband to check on his machines.

"Yeah, my wife was fucking your husband and they both ended up here." I winked my eye at her before leaving out the door.

I made it to the car in record time to find Sasha's stupid ass leaning against the car, shaking her leg like her nerves were bad. When she looked up at me she stood tall, expecting me to open her door. I hit the unlock button on my key fob and went to the driver's side and got in. That gentleman shit was over for her. She was nothing but a hoe to me.

Once we got to the house, she walked in before me. The entire ride home was quiet. I lit a blunt and made sure to blow the smoke her way because she hated that shit. She walked in the living room to the steps

"What is that smell, Draco?" she asked, coughing, and I laughed. I heard her footsteps as she walked to our master bedroom and I walked slow on purpose.

"What the fuck did you do?!" she yelled once she got to the room.

"You fucked that nigga on our bed so I set that bitch on fire. You better pack yo' shit and get the fuck out of this house before yo' fucking body gets burned next. Grab yo' keys and purse and get the fuck out, Sasha. This marriage is over," I told her as I walked away from her and out her fucking life.

Chapter 6
Jonah

Two months has passed since Sasha got shot. I still hadn't found a place for me and Paris to live yet because I really wanted Sasha's assistance because she's more familiar with what areas were good to live in. She'd been no help, though, because she'd been depressed as hell since Draco left her. Originally, he told her to get out but he couldn't stand being in that house after what happened, so he moved out and left it to her. Every time Sasha tried to call him, he ignored her. The only bright side of things was that he hadn't filed for a divorce so that made her believe there's still hope for her marriage.

I didn't know what'd been going on with Paris lately. I knew she started her internship and she's pregnant, but she'd been distant toward me. I didn't want to rush her into anything and I was starting to wonder if I was moving too fast. We never discussed moving in together and now I was practically living in her house. She hadn't said anything about it, but I could tell she was feeling some kind of way about it. I planned on sitting down with her this evening and discussing it with her.

She's five months now and we were supposed to go get an

ultrasound done today to find out the sex of the baby, but she told me that the appointment was canceled last minute.

I didn't know why, but something in my gut was telling me that she's lying. I didn't want to call her out on it and make it seem like I didn't trust her. I guess when I thought about it, she didn't really have a reason to lie. I mean, what woman wouldn't want the father of her child to go with her to find out the sex of their baby?

No lie, I was disappointed when I found out that there was no appointment today because this was what I'd been waiting for since I found out she was pregnant. I'm ready to start baby shopping already. That's really why I'm in a hurry to find a house so that way I could start on the nursery. Don't get me wrong, Paris's condo was nice as hell but it wasn't enough space for all of us. She had two bedrooms but one of them was her office. I needed an office of my own as well as a man cave to chill in. I'd always envisioned that once I had a kid it would be with a woman that I was going to marry. We'd live together and raise our child as a family. I shouldn't have to pick and choose what day I could see my child. That wouldn't be fair to either of us.

"Thanks for waiting up here for me. They wouldn't let me get the procedure done without them knowing someone was going to come pick me up afterward," Sasha said, walking up to me, breaking me away from my thoughts.

"No problem, sis, I gotcha," I told her as we walked out of the abortion clinic.

About a week after the shooting incident Sasha got a call from the hospital informing her that she was pregnant. She just knew the doctors had her mixed up with someone else, so she went to go take another test and it was confirmed. I tried to convince her to keep her baby then we could raise our kids together, but she wasn't trying to hear that. She didn't want kids and she definitely didn't want them by a man that wasn't her husband. I told her it was a chance that it could be Draco's, but she wasn't willing to take that chance. She would have got the abortion as soon as she found out, but she wanted to get the cast off her arm first. Now that she got rid of the baby, hopefully she'd get back to her normal self. I wasn't trying to be insensitive, but I needed my big sister to be there for me.

I drove Sasha to her house and sat there with her for a couple hours before going to Paris's condo. When I made it there her car was already in its designated parking spot. I parked next to it and climbed out. I headed up the stairs and rang Paris's doorbell. This was another sign that had me thinking she might not be ready for us to live here. I'd been staying with her since I found out about the pregnancy, and I still didn't have a key to her house. I had to ring the doorbell or call and let her know when I'm on my way. This didn't even feel like home to me but I'm paying the bills here and for my crib that I only saw once a month. I could afford to get a place on my own and still help Paris, but with us having a child together I felt like that's a waste of money. That money could be going toward a college fund for our child.

I lifted my hand to ring the doorbell, but she swung it open first. I gulped as my eyes gazed over her body. She was looking sexy as hell in a red teddy with a pair of red bottoms. She had gained a few pounds, but it was mostly in her thighs, ass, and stomach. Even at five months pregnant she made sure to work out and watch what she ate. I didn't even think it was possible for her to get more beautiful than she was before her pregnancy. She had a glow to her that would light up and dark room.

"Hey Daddy, are you coming in or do you want to give the neighbors a show?" she asked with a smirk.

"Damn girl, you sexy as hell," I replied as I walked in the

house. I pulled her close to me and kissed her passionately on the lips. My hands went to grip her ass but she stopped me.

"Not yet, I made dinner for us."

"Shit, I see my dinner right here in front of me."

"Nah baby, I'm your dessert. Now go wash your hands so we can eat," she told me, walking away with an extra switch to her hips.

I followed behind her with my eyes glued to her ass the entire time. I was definitely one lucky man to end up with a woman like Paris. I was forever in debt to Sasha for introducing me to Paris and having a hand in creating our first born. Paris was the full package. You'd be a damn fool not to fuck with a woman like her. Not only was she beautiful but she's smart, cooks, and makes sure to keep a clean house. I'm not even going to talk about how she's a freak in the bed. I'm older than her and I'm not ashamed to say she's taught me a few tricks in the bedroom. With my ex, she took the dick whatever way I gave it to her. She never took charge or told me how she really wanted it so hell, I didn't know if I was doing the shit right or not. Eventually I figured there must have been a problem being that she went and married my friend. Had she told me what the issue was I would have worked to rectify the situation and I would be the one married to her with kids right now.

I smiled as I looked at the layout Paris had planned. There were candles lit and the table was set with a bottle of champagne on ice. She turned on jazz to set the mood and I was wondering what was the occasion. I wanted to ask but I didn't want to ruin the mood. She instructed me to have a seat and I did as she said. Shortly after, she came out with plates of food. It all looked amazing. She cooked steak, shrimp, baked potatoes, and asparagus.

I popped the cork on the bottle as she sat down next to me.

"All of this looks amazing, baby," I told her with a smile.

"Thank you, I just wanted to do something to show my appreciation to you for being here for me. I know I'm not the easiest person to get along with right now. It's just this pregnancy took me by surprise and I'm still trying to adjust to it."

"You don't have to thank me, baby. I'm your man and it's my job to be here for you every step of the way. Just know that you'll never have to go through this pregnancy alone or worry about having help with our child."

"I know that and I'll forever be grateful for that. There's something that I need to tell you. I kind of lied about the ultrasound being canceled today."

There it was, my gut was never wrong. I took a deep breath to calm down before responding to her.

"Why did you lie, Paris? Who was you with?" I asked calmly.

"I didn't want to find out the sex of the baby. I wanted it to be a surprise so I had Robin go with me and they told her the gender. I knew if you went you were going to make them tell you. We're going to have a gender reveal and everyone will find out together," she explained.

"What the hell, Paris? You still should have told me. I would have gone so I could experience it."

"I didn't see what the big deal was. You already went with me to one ultrasound. This one was no different. I didn't think it was a big deal," she said nonchalantly.

"It was a big fucking deal, Paris. You knew I wanted to be there for that," I yelled, banging my fist on the table.

Just that quick, my anger had gotten the best of me.

Paris stood there looking at me for a minute, and I knew she was ready to go off on me. I opened my mouth to apologize, but it was too late.

"I don't know what the fuck your problem is, but chill out yelling at me like you done lost your mind. I spent my time cooking a hot meal and pampering myself so I can give you some pussy and this is the thanks I get? You'll see the next day I try to do something nice for your ass," Paris snapped as she walked away.

I hurriedly jumped from my seat and gently grabbed her from behind.

"I'm sorry, baby, I do appreciate what you did for me. I shouldn't have lost my temper. Please forgive me," I pleaded as I led her back over to the table. I really did want to sit and eat with her because we had some things to discuss.

Paris sighed before finally sitting down. She didn't look at me but instead started eating her food. I knew that she was still upset and I needed to change her mood quick or she wasn't going to give me none tonight, and after seeing her dressed like this, all I wanted to do was slide my dick inside of her.

After eating in silence for about ten minutes, I couldn't take it anymore.

"Paris, where do you see this relationship going?"

"What do you mean?" she asked, looking up at me.

"What I mean is I know that I love you and someday I want to make you my wife. We're having a kid together and I'm ready to take the next step, but I need to know if you're ready too."

"Are you asking me to marry you?" she inquired with a shocked look on her face.

"No, well, at least not right now but I will in the future. I want us to buy a house together so we can give our child a two-parent home. Our kid shouldn't have to live in between two houses."

"Where is this coming from all of a sudden?"

"How is this all of a sudden? I've been here with you damn near every day since I found out you were pregnant. You had to know that I expected us to live together."

Paris sat quiet for a minute. I'm guessing she was trying to figure out the right words to tell me I done lost my damn mind.

"I care about you deeply Jonah, but I just don't know if I'm ready to live with you. I've never lived with a man before and that's a big step."

"We're having a kid together, that is a big step. The reason I don't have any kids yet is because I said I wanted to wait until I was married. I never wanted to just be someone's baby daddy," I admitted, ignoring the fact that she still hadn't told me she loved me. I told her all the time and she'd always just kiss me or try to have sex in order to avoid the conversation.

"I understand where you're coming from, but neither of us planned this baby but now we have to live with it. Just because we're having a child doesn't mean we're forced to be together."

"So what are you saying, Paris? You don't want to be with me?"

"When did I say that? All I'm saying is I'm not ready to move in with you yet. We still have time, what's the rush?"

"I want to find something and have us moved in by the time the baby is born. This condo isn't big enough and I'm tired of paying for a mortgage somewhere else and rent here."

"I never asked you to pay the bills here. You chose to do that all on your own and I accepted it."

"The hell I look like laying up with you and not helping out? I don't know the type of niggas you're used to, but I wasn't raised like that," I said, feeling my blood pressure start to rise.

I could already tell this evening was not going to end the way I expected. Instead of us making love the rest of the night, we were butting heads on whether we should live together or not and how we should raise our child. I couldn't take it anymore so I left to go stay with Sasha for the night in hopes that she could give me some insight on what to do.

Chapter 7
Paris

I knew it was fucked up that I'd lied to Jonah, but what the fuck was I supposed to tell him? Tell him 'oh, I didn't want you to come because Draco came'? That nigga would have knocked my shit loose. Just from me saying that Robin went with me instead made him damn near knock all the food from the table. That in itself displayed that he had anger issues and I knew I couldn't deal with that shit. That nigga could think he gon' flash out on me, but he bleed just like I bleed. I'd thump it out with his ass before I let him play with me like that.

In my heart of hearts, I knew this wasn't Jonah's baby but I couldn't let him go. Shit just felt different with Draco. It was easy. Draco came and went like a thief in the night. I couldn't even count on how many fingers that Draco came into my condo in the middle of the night just to fuck me or eat my pussy. Sometimes while Jonah was asleep or if he was at his own home.

It was like Draco had a fucking sixth sense or some shit. He knew just when to pop the fuck out. Granted, I was doing a gender reveal that was scheduled two days from now, but shit didn't feel real with Jonah. The dick was good and he thought he was paying the bills, but he wasn't. All the money he gave me went into an account that neither he nor Draco knew about. I made a vow to myself that when I left New Orleans, I wasn't coming back, and I would make the type of money that made a broke bitch sick. Hit a lick that made bitches and niggas sick. I didn't think that I would end up pregnant by a married man and fucking his brother-in-law to cover up our tracks. I was over this shit and over both of them.

I liked the way shit went with me and Draco because we didn't live together. Jonah was starting to crowd my space and I didn't care for that. He was talking living together and marriage when I didn't even feel the same way. I liked him but I wasn't in love with him. I didn't want to lead him on and hurt his feelings, but he was becoming a little too aggressive. I didn't want to move in with him and I def didn't want him staying with me.

"The fuck you over there overthinking shit fa?" Draco snapped me out my thoughts as he weaved through traffic. I felt like a high school girl cheating on her boyfriend. Per usual, he texted my phone asking me to come outside and to wear a dress. He knew I hated dresses now that I was pregnant because my stomach was big as fuck for me to be five months. I hated wearing panties so that was a no-go. Draco must have known I needed some of his dick because he was right on time. I know y'all probably thinking I'mma hoe, but I'm not. I make Jonah strap up. He hates it because I'm already pregnant, but I didn't care. I had a few slipups with him and that's why he thinks he's the father. I never used protection with Draco.

"Nothing, just life and the curve balls it throws," I said in a huff but being honest. I was in my fucking prime but pregnant.

"You better pick that bitch up and throw it back," he told me seriously, "You have everything you need and you know I got you, so stop trying to control the shit that you can't and go with the flow." He grabbed my hand and kissed the back of it. That was easier said than done. He made the shit sound so easy. When his lips touched the back of my hand I basked in his warm lips touching my skin and closed my eyes for a few seconds. It's was times like this that made me say fuck the world and we could just run off and never come back, but that wasn't our reality.

"I know you been fucking that nigga, but you better make his simple ass strap up," he said as if reading my thoughts, "I'm the only nigga fucking my pussy raw," he said, gripping my pussy while driving. His middle finger grazed my clit, making me shift in my seat. I arched my back and he slid his finger in my wet tunnel. He removed his finger that was wet with my juices and sucked it dry.

"Yo' shit taste so good." He laughed and continued to drive. I had been dying to ask him what went down at home, but I'd been beating around the questions because I didn't want him to become upset.

"Bae," I called him like he was far away. My pussy was screaming out for him to massage it.

"You saying my name and shit like I'm going somewhere and you know I ain't," he said, giving me that sexy ass one-sided smile. "You the one hurting that nigga feelings by not telling him the truth. He dumb as a box of fucking rocks to think that's his baby and you make him strap up," he laughed cockily, and I rolled my eyes. I had slipped up with Jonah but Draco was right, this was his baby. "He really a real-life clown performing in his own fucking circus."

I had to laugh at that because it was the truth. I didn't want to hurt Jonah, but it was inevitable. I lifted my body, pulling my dress above my stomach, sitting my bare ass on his seat. He glanced over at me and licked his lips. I slid the seat back to my liking and put both my legs on the dashboard wide open. I slid my hand between legs, letting my fingers do the talking. I felt the car swerve and knew Draco's eyes were on me hard.

"Don't fucking do that, P, you know I can't handle that shit." His eyes got lazy like he'd just blown a 'gar of gas. I had been with Draco since Jonah wanted to be childish and leave to run to Sasha and Draco ran to me. We'd spent the day shopping for my perfect dress for the gender reveal. Draco was the only one who knew the gender and that nigga wasn't giving up nothing. His face showed no emotion. My pussy couldn't even get that nigga to tell me the gender of my baby.

"If you want some dick, say that, but I ain't telling you what we having," he laughed, and I blew out an exhausted breath. "I told yo' ass you can't mind fuck me Paris, but you can sit on this dick," he said, and I rolled my eyes because I was mad, but he gotta know I was about to ride his big black dick in this car.

"Why you playing with me like that, P?" he asked me, tucking in his bottom lip.

"I want you to play with me, Daddy." The sex dripped from my voice as my index and middle slid in and out my tunnel. I wanted that dick and now.

"Damn P." I watched as his dick rose for the occasion through his joggers.

I didn't know what he had planned before we went to the reveal but whatever it was, I was down for it. We had the entire park blocked off and decorated with pink and blue balloons. Even the food was pink and blue. Because Jonah was mad, I didn't ask for his assistance with anything. I did that shit by myself. He called begging and pleading the next day talking about he could cover the expenses of the gender reveal, but I told him I had it covered. Draco popped up the morning of the reveal and we'd been together all day. We pulled into an underground garage. I looked around then at him.

"What the hell is this, Draco?" I wasn't scared because I knew he wouldn't hurt me.

"This where I live now," he told me, his eyes giving me a twice over, and he continued, "The bitch Sasha fucking over me for a nigga at work and had the fucking nerve to fuck the nigga in our bed," he blurted, and there it was.

That's why he told me to make Jonah stay home for the ultrasound, and that's why we were together now. The irony of this shit. But I gotta admit, Sasha a bold bitch to fuck a nigga in their bed, even I ain't that bold. My fucking confidence ain't that high with Jonah. I know what y'all thinking. Trust me when I say, me and Jonah have fucked in every part of that condo but my bed. I may have slipped up one time, but Draco made me cut that shit off. Jonah could only sleep in it, not fuck me in it.

"I set the bed on fire before telling that bitch to pack what she came in this fucking marriage with and get the fuck out before I burned her too," he said, and my face frowned. "Nah, don't give me that shit. I left Sasha because not only did she cheat, but in my house and left the cum spot. I would have forgiven her for cheating because I'm fucking with you, but in my house was the ultimate disrespect. I had to cause some type of destruction."

He laughed, but I ain't find shit funny. I'd mentioned to Jonah to not forget about Sasha because she had a hand in helping with the décor and catering, and I didn't want her to miss this moment. Now that I thought about it, she was kinda acting distant when we were shopping. Not because of me but her mind was in another space. Now it made perfect sense.

"What the fuck, Draco? You did too much like the fuck we not fucking," I told him.

"But can you ever fucking say that you know what the

inside of my home looks like?" He cocked he head to the side, looking at me, and I nodded my head no.

"Exactly my fucking point, that's the difference," he said and pulled his dick out. "Now come ride this dick in the Ferrari because we never fucked in here," he said and reclined the seat back, and I hopped on his dick reverse cowgirl position and went for a ride.

Once we finished being nasty, we took the elevators to the eighth floor with his hand wrapped around my waist.

"I don't want this shit to ever end," he whispered in my ear, and goosebumps formed on my skin because I didn't want it to end either.

"It won't," I told him as he kissed my shoulder, and I fell into the moment. The elevator doors opened and it was beautiful. My clothes had been brought to his condo along with a personal stylist and nail tech to get me glammed up. I turned around and jumped in his arms, wrapping my legs around his waist. I kissed him all over his face as he laughed.

"Come on, you have two hours to get dressed and to the park," he said, letting me down.

I walked away and followed him to the bathroom where he had candles lit and rose petals in the tub. He slowly undressed me and placed me inside.

"I got you," he said before walking away and letting me handle my business.

After an hour and a half, my hair was in an abundance of curls pulled to the side with a pink and blue diamond-encrusted barrette holding it together. My pink and blue encrusted dress hugged my body like a glove and stopped just above my knee. On my feet were pink and blue Gucci slides. I had a light beat with blue and pink glitter on my eyelids. I looked in the mirror at myself and smiled because I felt beautiful.

"Damn," I heard from behind me. I turned around to find Draco donned with a pink Gucci button down with linen blue shorts. He was handsome as fuck. I walked over and hugged him.

"How are we gonna show up together?" I asked him.

"The fuck you mean? We gon' get in the car, drive to the park, and get the fuck out the car, that's how." He said it and meant it. He grabbed my phone and purse with his keys and led me to the elevator.

I was on pins and needles the entire time he drove because that shit would look crazy. Granted, I didn't have much family, but all his friends would be there and they would talk. They didn't know the entire situation, but Jonah and Sasha did and I knew Jonah was about to act a fool. We pulled up to the park after thirty minutes of driving, and Draco pulled up to the front and got out. He came around to open the door for me and grabbed my hand, and I got out to walk on the grass.

"To your left there is your chair, which is fit for a queen. You sit there and I got the rest," he said and left me to go back in the car. I walked over and watched everyone as they watched me walk over to the chair. They acted as if I didn't just get out the car with Draco.

"Come on babes, let me take you to your seat." Sasha was the first to approach me, followed by Jonah. I was confused or maybe they knew some shit that I didn't know. It was weird but I played along. There was a cake table and other tables decorated for the guests to sit. It was packed to say that I didn't know half these people.

"I wanted this day to be special," Jonah whispered in my ear, and I smiled. He was a sweet nigga, just not the nigga for me.

Through the reveal, they catered to my every need. I didn't have to lift a finger. Everybody mingled and enjoyed themselves and indulged in the blunts and alcohol of their choice. It was time for the reveal and I was so excited. I had to damn near sell my soul to Draco and he still didn't tell me. I stood up as everybody moved to the big parking lot. Draco walked my way and grabbed my left hand and walked me to where everyone else was. Sasha was happy and that bothered me, because I knew a bitter woman when I saw one but it wasn't toward me. She smiled at me from my right side as we stopped on the concrete. I looked up and saw a silver Porsche revving the engine.

"That's Jonah in the car and when he pulls off the dust is going to fly in the air," Sasha said, a little too happy for my liking. I looked at Draco and he licked his lips.

Vrrroooommm

Jonah pulled off and the dust revealed pink and blue dust, and I was confused.

"P, we having fucking twins." Draco picked me up hugging me, forgetting where the fuck we were.

"Put me down, Draco," I whispered in his ear, and he did without bullshit this time. I turned to Sasha and hugged her as Jonah walked up all excited and shit, making me mad.

"Bae, we got two babies in this oven." He lifted me and I wrapped my arms around his neck to make the shit look real. I even kissed him for emphasis. I caught Draco's face and he made his hand like a gun, pulling the trigger to Jonah's head that only I could see. I mouthed no to him as he smirked and walked off to get a drink. I knew a war was brewing, but I just hoped there weren't any casualties.

Chapter 8
Draco

My blood started boiling when I saw Paris kissing Jonah like I wasn't just deep in her guts a couple hours ago. I didn't want to make a scene in front of everybody so I took a deep breath then went to get me a drink. I had to figure out a way to tell Paris to leave Jonah alone without sounding like some lame.

The truth was I could dish out cheating and fucking other women but I couldn't handle the fact of knowing one of my bitches was sleeping with someone else. That's one of the main reasons why I hadn't gone back to Sasha. Every time I'm around her all I could think about was her fucking and sucking that nigga. Just thinking about it made me want to go back to that hospital and finish what I started. I didn't know if he had kids but I knew he had a wife and she didn't deserve to morn her husband. As much as I couldn't stand Sasha's ass right now I wouldn't want her dead.

I'm at the point where I didn't even know if our marriage was salvageable. I mean, what the hell was the purpose of me fighting for it when I knew she'd never forgive me once she found out that Paris's twins were mine. I'd been debating on just ripping the Band-Aid off now and telling Sasha. I owed her and Paris that much. The only thing that stopped me was I didn't want to fuck things up for Paris. I knew if I told Sasha then she was going to tell Jonah. The last thing I needed right now was Paris being stressed out, because I'd fuck everybody up behind my kids.

I knocked back a shot of Henny then looked over at Jonah and Paris smiling while everyone congratulated them. It was taking everything in me not to go over there and snatch her ass up. I wanted to shout it out to the world that those were my motherfucking kids but instead, I'm sitting here like a lame ass nigga playing the background.

If someone would have warned me that day when I approached Paris that I would fall in love with her and get her pregnant, I would have stayed in my damn car. It was never supposed to get to this point. When I proposed to Sasha I had plans on spending the rest of my life with her. I couldn't even blame Sasha, though, because this was all on me. I caused all my own problems. I couldn't even get mad at Paris because I was supposed to be loyal to my wife. Paris didn't owe me or Sasha shit. If I was a better man I'd let Paris run off with Jonah, but I couldn't do that. Maybe if kids weren't involved I would. Nah, I'm lying, because I loved Paris too much. I couldn't help but be selfish with her. I'd been thinking a lot lately though. Since I didn't see a future with Sasha anymore, I'm thinking of finally sending her the divorce papers so I could make things official with Paris. These last couple of months things had been great between me and Paris. I'm not just talking about the sex either. There's a new connection between us and I couldn't explain it. I wanted to wake up and go to sleep with her every night.

The condo I had had four bedrooms in it because I bought it with Paris and our unborn child in mind. I wanted to be able to see my kids grow up in the same home as me. That was something that I'd never experienced. Paris's condo was cool but it's not big enough for her and two kids. I knew I needed to shoot my shot before she decided to get a house with Jonah. I planned all this thinking it was only one child but now that it's two, this was beneficial for both of us. I couldn't allow her to try and raise two kids on her own.

"What the hell is going on between you and Paris?" Sasha asked, pulling me from my thoughts. I was so caught up with paying attention to Paris and Jonah that I didn't see her walk up.

"What the fuck are you talking about?" I asked, finally looking her in the eyes. I could tell that she had been drinking because her eyes were low. She wasn't really a drinker so that meant she was about to get on demon time.

"You heard me. Are y'all fucking or something? I'm not stupid, Draco. I see the way you look at her. This isn't the first time I peeped it either. I saw how you were the first time I introduced them. Is that why you didn't want her with anyone because you were sticking your dick in her?"

Sasha was getting loud and I could see people starting to look in our direction. I didn't like people in my business and this was not the place for this conversation. I wasn't about to allow her to ruin this moment for me. In spite of everything that's going on I'm happy as hell to know that Paris was having my kids. I'm about to have a son and a daughter so if I never had kids again, I'm fine with that. This was two more than I thought I'd ever have anytime soon.

"Sasha, sit your drunk ass down somewhere. You're tripping right now over nothing. She has no family and she works for me. I told her that I'd look out for her and that's all I'm doing. Paris and I are just friends. Don't try to turn shit around on me because you got caught."

"I might be drunk but I'm not stupid, Draco. I might have got caught but I didn't start this shit. You've cheated on me so many times that I've lost count, with numerous bitches, but the one time I do something you leave without even allowing me to explain."

"What the fuck was there to explain? There was no way you could talk your way out of that bullshit. I may have done my dirt in the past, but not one bitch can say they know what the inside of our crib looks like," I bellowed, causing everyone to look in our direction. Just that quick we had caused a scene.

I got up from the bar, heading toward my car with Sasha hot on my trail. I was hoping she would just take her ass home and leave me the fuck alone. She had me ready to start spazzing on her ass.

"Stop, don't walk away from me when I'm talking to you," Sasha yelled, grabbing me by my arm.

I snatched away from her and she fell flat on her ass. I looked down at her for a minute before finally helping her up off the ground. I opened the passenger door and pushed her inside before walking over to the driver's seat. I didn't want to be anywhere near Sasha but I couldn't let her drive home in this condition, and I definitely didn't need her approaching Paris.

Sasha tried to protest but I wasn't trying to hear her. I blasted the music on the radio and it was like that the entire thirty-minute drive to my old house. I got out of the car and helped Sasha out. I used my key and led her into the house. Just being here had me ready to burn this bitch to the ground with Sasha in it.

"You should be good from here," I said, turning to walk away.

"Please, don't leave me, Draco. I'm tired of being here alone. What can I do to fix this? I've forgiven you for everything you've done but you can't forgive me? Do you even love me like you claimed you did?" she cried.

"I'll always love you Sasha and I can maybe even forgive you someday, but I can't right now. I can't stand to look at you right now," I confessed.

"Where are you staying? Are you laying up at some bitch's house? I went to your old apartment that you thought I didn't know about but your car is never there."

I sighed as I sat down in the chair across from her. That was another reason why I moved so quickly because I didn't need Sasha popping up out of the blue while I was chilling with Paris.

"I don't live in the old apartment and I don't stay with a bitch. I'm renting out a condo," I lied. I didn't want her to know that I had bought it just in case things didn't work out with Paris the way I wanted it to.

"Is it really over between us, Draco? Do you want a divorce? We could try marriage counseling."

"You know I don't like putting people in my business. I just need some space right now to clear my head while I figure out what to do about us."

"How much time do you need? This shit is pure torture. I miss you so fucking much. How can you not miss me?"

"I do miss you Sasha, but I can't go there with you right now. Being in this house makes me want to knock you upside your shit or better yet, finish that nigga off."

"What if we get a new house? Do you think we'll have a chance then?"

I was about to reply when my phone buzzed. I looked down at it and saw that it was Paris. I debated on whether to answer it not. I didn't know if something had happened so I picked up.

"Hey, is everything okay?"

"Yeah, what happened to you? You left without saying anything and my keys are at your house."

"Sasha had been drinking so I brought her home. I'm about to leave now though to come pick you up."

"That's okay, Jonah is on his way to Sasha's house so I'll have Robin drop me off."

"Okay, I'll be there in a minute," I told her before hanging up.

"Who was that?" Sasha asked.

"Paris, she left her keys in my car."

"Are you serious right now, Draco? We were in the middle of a conversation and now you're about to just run out to give her some damn keys."

"She's pregnant Sasha, it's not like I can just leave her to stand outside on her own."

"Why did you bring her to start off with?"

"Her and your brother have been having problems and I didn't want her driving herself so I volunteered to pick her up. After all, she's carrying our niece and nephew," I said with the straightest face possible. This was the first and last time I would ever refer to them as that.

"Whatever nigga, if I find out you were having an affair with that bitch, I will make both of your lives a living hell."

"Bitch, watch your motherfucking mouth. You already know I don't take threats well."

"Is everything alright in here?" Jonah asked from behind us.

"Yeah, we good, nigga," I responded.

"What's your problem with me, Draco? You act like we got beef or something," Jonah said as if he was about that life. He had me ready to rock his ass.

"He wants your bitch, Jonah. If he ain't fucked Paris yet, he wants to," Sasha slurred.

"Man, I don't have time for this shit. I told your ass I ain't did shit with that girl," I bellowed like I was mad. I was putting on a full show for them and since they both wanted to be on bullshit, I was about to make Paris stay with me tonight so I could beat the pussy up all night while they sat here and bitched and moaned about whether I was fucking Paris or not.

By the time I made it to my crib Paris was sitting outside in the car with Robin. I knocked on the window, causing them to jump.

"What the hell, Draco?" Paris huffed.

"I'm sorry, but you should have been paying attention to your surroundings. Come on so we can go inside the house."

Paris told Robin goodbye then followed me in the building. We got on the elevator and rode it upstairs. As soon as we were in the house I wrapped my arms around Paris.

"Stoppp, you're squashing me," Paris whined.

"My bad, I'm just excited that we're having twins. Thank you so much for making this happen. I know it's not ideal, but I promise we're going to make it work, Paris. I love you so fucking much."

"I love you too, Draco," Paris replied before kissing me passionately on the lips. It was one of those kisses that made my dick stand at attention. I was ready to bend her over and give her what she wanted, but it was only right that I warned her about Sasha.

"Baby, wait, there's something I need to tell you."

"What is it?"

"Sasha confronted me today and asked if we were fucking."

"What the hell Draco, this is your fault. I told you we shouldn't have rode together to the gender reveal."

"I hate to break it to you but she's been suspicious for a while."

"So what now? This is so fucked up."

"We're just going to continue to live our lives like we've

been doing. She don't have any proof and if she did, I don't give a fuck because once we get a DNA test done she's going to know we were fucking."

"You know it's not too late for us to keep this to ourselves. We don't have to get a test done. I told you we can pretend these are Jonah's kids and you can work on your marriage. You could see the twins when you want. You can be the cool uncle or better yet, I can make you the godfather."

"Do I look like some simple ass nigga to you, Paris? Let that be the last time you let that shit come out of your mouth."

"Okay, I'm sorry baby. I was just trying to make your life easier."

"My life is easy as long as you're in it," I told her before placing my lips on hers. I was ready to pick up from where we left off earlier.

Chapter 9
Paris
4 months later

At this point I felt fucking stupid. It was one thing to actually be stupid for a nigga and let it show, but I felt stupid on the inside, which meant this shit had to come to an end. If my mother knew what the fuck I was into, she would be saying I told you so. She didn't even know I was pregnant. I felt like I was being stupid for Draco because I was doing shit that I knew went against what the fuck I believed in. I shouldn't have even signed up for this shit because I came second to no one. Although he didn't treat me that way, he still had a wife at home. I didn't do married fucking men until now and look at the shit that's going on.

After I left Draco, I tried my best to stay away from him, but he always popped up everywhere I went. Two weeks after the gender reveal, I was placed on bed rest because of the risk of me delivering early. The twins were big as hell inside of me and taking up too much space. I had to limit my activities from day to day. That didn't stop me from moving because once Draco texted me to meet him outside, I came running whether Jonah was there or not. He was trying his best to change my mind about moving in with him but he couldn't. My mind was too strong for Jonah. I could run circles around him, and that's putting it lightly.

Jonah was a good man, without a doubt, but he wasn't the man for me and I couldn't force it. I tried because he was sweet in the beginning, but it's like something clicked in this nigga's head. One night me and Draco were texting, and he whined and yanked the phone out of my hand. I grabbed the fucking lamp and threw it at him because he didn't pay my fucking phone bill. He threw my phone to the floor and left like I was supposed to be pissed. All I did was waddle to where my phone was and call Draco. He came to pick me up and took me to his new condo. I didn't want to call him but who else could I call? I could have called Sasha but the bitch was so fixated on me and Draco fucking that I was scared the bitch would try some shit to harm me and my babies. I heard the door open and Draco walked in. He looked at me before looking by the sofa, noticing the broken lamp. He stormed toward where I sat pulling a dress over my head.

"This nigga did this shit?" he asked me but kept talking before I could respond, "You see why the fuck I said Jonah got some shit loose in his head? Now you fucking see," he yelled at me before helping me pull the dress over my belly.

"Draco, stop that yelling. I broke the fucking lamp because he took my phone from me." I mushed his head because this shit was his fault. "If I wouldn't have been texting yo' ass and ignoring him then this shit wouldn't have happened," I told him before standing to my feet.

"This shit is getting out of hand and I don't like it. This shit ain't good for my health, Draco. You want me to play nice with a nigga that I don't want while I'm nine months pregnant with yo' kids, nigga!!" I threw my phone in his face. I was tired. Tired of this façade we were putting on, tired of lying to Sasha and Jonah, just tired of being fucking pregnant.

"You know these are yo' babies but you want a fucking DNA test to prove it? To make yo' wife mad? Or to drive Jonah mad because he thinks these are his kids?!" I yelled in his face, and he backed up. I was ready for all this shit to be over with. If I thought I could travel, I would hop on a plane to New Orleans on some secret shit and not look back, but Draco would find me. I felt like my life was trapped in a fucking box with Draco and Jonah on each end. Sasha wasn't even a part of the equation because no woman intimidated me. Her husband wanted me, not the other way around.

"Don't try to turn this shit on me, Paris. It was you who wanted the DNA test. Make Sasha mad for what? Our marriage is fucking over, but don't change yo' mind now. We getting the fucking DNA test so that nigga can look foolish," he told me, and I closed my mouth because he was stating all facts.

"You think I planned my fucking life like this, Paris? Sasha was my forever but you came along and shook some shit up." He smirked and smiled, making my heart sink. "You think I wanted to involuntarily give my fucking heart to another woman when it was supposed to be in my wife's possession? Yeah, I cheated on Sasha in the fucking past but I stopped, then you came along and changed everything about me. You made me realize what I couldn't see, and that was love. Not just loving someone but being in fucking love. You got my fucking heart in yo' pocket, girl. Do you know the sick, twisted shit that run across my mind with the thought of Jonah touching or fucking you? I could kill that nigga and help Sasha plan his fucking funeral," he barked at me, and I didn't move. All that shit sounded good but without action behind it, it didn't mean shit. I wanted to kiss him, wrap my arms around him, and tell him how I wanted to be his. Be his person like I had been since meeting him, but I couldn't. I could scream to the mountain tops that I was his but when the dust settled, he still belonged to someone else.

"You have given me something that my wife would never give me." He took steps forward and I backed up. His hands rubbed my stomach and both babies started to kick, making my knees weak. "You never once said you wanted an abortion when you found out you were pregnant, but when I called one of my hittas, I found out that Sasha had a fucking abortion. You know how the fuck that made me feel? To know that she fucked that nigga raw and actually got fucking pregnant and thought that she could hide that shit from me? You have no idea when I have been begging this bitch to have a baby for me, her fucking husband, for almost four fucking years?!" he stated calmly but deadly. "That bitch is dead to me now, she for the streets," he said and backed away from me. "But I get it. I really do get it. I put you in this position of having to pretend and lie about what the fuck is going on, and that's on me. You went along with the shit because of me and I let the shit go on for too long." My heart started to thump out my chest because I didn't know what the fuck he was saying. Was he about to say 'fuck me' and move on? Was he about to try to make shit work with his wife? I started to feel insecure and pulled at the bottom of my dress.

"Don't clam up on me, Paris. You know I don't play that insecure shit. You ain't been insecure so don't start it now. I'm saying I need to clean my own shit up and I'm sorry for bringing this into your life." I felt the tears in the rim of my eyes with each word he spoke.

"You didn't bring nothing into my life without me allowing you to," I told him. That's the shit that made me feel stupid. I felt like I was excusing what the fuck we were doing even though it was wrong. I was allowing all this shit to go on instead of stopping it.

"Just go, Draco," I told him, pushing him to the door. I didn't need this stress. I was ready to go to bed. I knew Jonah like the back of my hand. If he was mad, then nine times outta ten he wasn't coming back until tomorrow, which was fine by me. "Somebody will call you if shit happens, I'm sure of it," I told him, and he didn't put up a fight. He turned his back to me and walked away. I was glad he left without a fuss because I was exhausted.

After he left, I shut the door, making sure to lock it. As I walked over to the bed I pulled my dress off and got comfortable in my bed. I loved to sleep naked since becoming pregnant. It gave me a sense of peace that I couldn't describe. I grabbed my remote and turned it to *Good Times* until I began to nod off. I must have nodded off heavy because when I opened my eyes, Jonah was standing at the foot of my bed. I pulled the cover that fell over my belly to cover the top half and sat up.

"What the fuck are you staring at me for? You thinking about killing me or some shit?" I laughed a little because he was giving me a deranged look. As if snapping out of it, he walked closer to me and out of habit, I swung my legs to the floor in case he tried some stupid shit. A smile touched his lips but didn't meet his eyes.

"Nah, I came back to apologize because I left on some bitch shit. I knew you were here alone and due any day now, so I came back," he said and sat on side of me. "Fuck, I never really left. I got to my car and felt fucked up about what happened and decided not to leave. To just cool off for a minute. I was about to walk back up when I saw Draco parking his whip," he said, and I was about to speak but he stopped me. "Ain't no sweat because I knew how long he was up here. I knew you were texting him but I ain't stupid, I knew he was gon' fall through." He grabbed my had and looked at me. "But don't let that shit happen again." Before I could respond I felt a hard ass kick then my thighs felt wet.

"Aaaggghhhhhhh!!!" I screamed as I looked at Jonah, and he panicked. I opened my thighs wide because my coochie felt like it was opening up.

"These fucking babies are coming Jonah, where is my bag?!" I screamed in horror because I didn't think this shit would happen right now. He was shook. He couldn't fucking move. When I tried to stand was when he came back to earth.

"Where is your bag, Paris?" he shouted, almost blowing my fucking eyebrows off.

I pointed to my closet. "Get my dress off the floor and help me put it on." He didn't know which way to go. Another pain hit me and I screamed.

"Let me call Sasha to help," he said, and I yanked his phone from him. Another pain hit and I couldn't speak, but my mind was saying no. I gripped the bed rail and his wrist, dropping his phone.

"Drraaccoooo," I yelled through the pain. My teeth grinded as I tried to stop the pain.

"I'm here with you trying to call help and that's the nigga's name you call?" he asked, perplexed. It came out all wrong. I didn't fucking know Sasha for her to be the first one I called when my water broke. She wasn't my fucking friend and I wasn't about to pretend with my babies on their way. The pain subsided and I took that time to stand to my feet and talk to him.

"I don't know yo' fucking sister. I know Draco, so why the fuck would you call her? I'm Draco's friend, not hers," I told him, out of breath. "And do what the fuck I tell you to do, the fuck wrong with you!" I screamed as another contraction hit me. I looked on the bed at my phone and grabbed it to call Draco since his simple ass wouldn't.

"You don't see the bigger fucking picture, Paris. How the fuck would that look if I called Draco before Sasha?" He was trying to be calm, but I knew that was a low blow but I didn't give a fuck. I said what I said.

"I don't give a fuck about a bigger picture or the fucking camera, Jonah, I said call Draco and you still haven't. You wanna argue with me even while I'm in labor and wonder why the fuck I don't wanna move in with you," I yelled at him as another gush of water came down my legs. I didn't give a fuck who he called but I needed to get to the fucking hospital before my babies fell out of me and onto the floor. I tried to grab my phone but my other hand slipped under my dress. My body felt weak. Something was wrong. I pulled my hand back and noticed the blood dripping from it. I looked at Jonah with the bag wrapped around the front of his body. If he wasn't fucking fussing I would have been at the hospital. I looked at my phone, dialing Draco.

"Draco, I need you. The babies are coming" I yelled into the phone, bending over in pain. I noticed the blood on the floor and became weaker.

"I got you," I heard Jonah say before I felt myself falling asleep and being carried out the condo.

Chapter 10
Jonah

My heart dropped as I caught Paris in my arms. There was blood all over her dress and that scared the hell out of me.

"Paris. What the hell, Paris. Why aren't you answering me?" Draco yelled through her phone. I couldn't talk to him and carry Paris at the same time, so I grabbed her phone and scooped her up in my arms. I made my way to my car as fast as I could.

I put her in the back seat then hopped in the driver seat and drove off. A minute passed before her phone started ringing. I looked down at it and saw that it was Draco. As much as I didn't want to talk to him, he was the one that Paris wanted me to call and I didn't want her mad at me. I also didn't know what to do and I didn't want to deal with this alone.

"Hello," I answered.

"Where the hell is Paris? Why do you have her phone?"

"Her water broke and she passed out. Something is wrong with her. There was a lot of blood. We're headed to the hospital by her house now."

"Okay, I'm on my way," he said before handing up.

I put Paris's phone away and called Sasha. I needed my sister there with me. I knew Paris said not to call her but she's my sister, and if Draco could be there I didn't see why Sasha couldn't.

I pulled up to the emergency room and ran inside.

"I need somebody to help me. My pregnant girlfriend passed out and she's bleeding," I announced.

The receptionist called for a doctor and they came rushing out with a gurney. I led the way to my car and they took her out. By the time they got her out of my car Draco was running up. I had no idea how he made it here so fast. He must've never left the area when he left Paris's condo.

I went to search for a park while Draco walked inside of the hospital. I circled the lot for five minutes before I finally found a parking spot. I jogged back to the emergency room and when I made it there, all I saw was the receptionist at the desk.

"Hey, where's the pregnant girl that I brought in?"

"They rushed her upstairs for an emergency cesarean."

"Okay, I need to be up there with her. Can you tell me what floor it's on?"

"Unfortunately, she already has one person with her. There's only one visitor allowed during a cesarean."

"Well tell him to leave, I'm the father of the baby."

"I'm sorry, but it's too late. You're going to have to wait in the waiting room on our surgery floor. You can let them know that you're waiting for her condition and they'll keep you updated."

"Man, this is some bullshit," I grumbled before walking to the elevator and heading upstairs. I stopped at the desk and gave my information then went inside of the waiting room. I saw Paris's name on the board and saw that they started on her surgery already. I couldn't fucking believe Draco was actually in there while my babies were being born and I was sitting out here in the waiting room. I didn't know what type of shit they on, but I'm going to get to the bottom of it.

Forty-five minutes passed when Sasha walked inside of the visiting room.

"What are you doing in here? Aren't you supposed to be in the procedure room with Paris?"

"I would be if your husband wasn't in there with her."

"What the hell are you taking about? Why would Draco be here?"

"Paris told me to call him. He showed up here and while I was parking he went upstairs with her."

"You didn't think it was suspicious that she wanted Draco at the hospital during her delivery?" Sasha asked.

I sighed because I didn't know if I should tell her that Draco was at Paris's house earlier. Maybe I should tell her everything I knew. I didn't have proof, though, so she probably wouldn't even believe me.

"She said that Draco and her were close due to her working with him. Before I could ask any other questions she had passed out. There was blood and I freaked out, so I told him where we were," I said, telling half the truth.

Sasha and I talked for another forty minutes before someone finally called and told me she was out of surgery. I still had to wait twenty minutes for her to get done with recovery before I could go see her. Those were the longest twenty minutes of my life. I was anxious to see Paris and my twins. I wondered if they looked like either of us yet. I knew it was wishful thinking since they were barely a couple hours old, but I couldn't help but have those thoughts.

Once the twenty minutes passed Sasha and I headed upstairs to Paris's room. When we walked inside Paris was asleep and Draco was sitting beside her holding my damn kids like they were his. He had a look in his eyes that I didn't recognize. I had never seen him look that way before. It was almost as if it was pride and joy, which confused me even more since they didn't belong to him.

"What happened? Why is she still sleeping?" I asked.

"She's still sedated right now. Her placenta ruptured but they were able to stabilize her and the bleeding. They're not sure if she'll be able to have any more kids," Draco replied.

"Damn, does she know?"

"Yeah, the surgeon told her in recovery."

"Okay, well can I at least see my kids?" I asked sarcastically.

Draco hesitantly handed them over to me. They were both light skin with a head full of curly hair. They really didn't have any features yet, which was to be expected.

Paris started stirring in her sleep and Draco immediately was by her side. I didn't care what neither of them said. There was no way anyone could convince me that they weren't fucking. Draco didn't even care about Sasha being in the room with us.

"Hey, are my babies okay?" Paris asked.

"Yeah, they're fine, Jonah is holding them over there," Draco replied.

Paris turned and looked my way with a half smile on her face.

"Can I see my kids?" she asked.

"Of course," I told her as I handed her the twins. She looked down at them and smiled before examining them. I had no idea what it was she was looking for, but all of a sudden her mood had changed.

"Hey, I see we have a full room," a Hispanic nurse said as she walked into the room.

"We know there's only supposed to be two people but we wanted to make sure she's alright."

"That's understandable, but you all only have five minutes

then you all have to go. Only the father is allowed to stay," she said.

"Okay, that's fine. My sister and brother-in-law will be leaving in a couple minutes," I assured her.

"Actually, before you leave, I wanted to know what is the process of getting a DNA test done?" Paris spoke up, causing me to look in her direction.

"The fuck you need a DNA test for?" I asked.

"You know we weren't exclusive when we started sleeping together. I just want to make sure the kids are yours before we go any further."

"You don't think you could have waited until we were alone to bring this up?"

"What? You were living in a different state and I was horny. I had sex with someone else right before you came to town for my birthday," she stated as if it was that simple.

"And you waited until now to say something? I fucking talked to you about me wanting to spend my life with you and it never crossed your mind to tell me these might not be my kids?"

"Look, don't act like I led you on or some shit. I told you that I wasn't ready for what you were. Hence the reason I didn't move into a house with you."

"Uhm, Draco, maybe we should go so they can talk in private," Sasha suggested.

Draco stood there as if Sasha wasn't talking to her.

"Yeah, maybe y'all should leave so Paris and I can finish this up," I added.

"Man, if I didn't listen to Sasha say it what makes you think you repeating it gone make me move?"

The nurse looked at all of us like she didn't know what to do or say.

"It's okay, Dray, me and the kids are fine. Visiting hours

start in the morning at 9. You can come back then," Paris tried to convince him.

"Okay, call me if you need anything before then."

"Really Draco? That's all it took? Are you going to act like I'm not standing here?" Sasha yelled.

"I'm sorry, but Mom just went through a major surgery. I'm going to need y'all to leave because she doesn't need to be stressed out," the nurse stepped in.

"Paris, are you and my husband fucking? Is he the other possible father of your kids?" Sasha asked.

"You don't have to answer that, Paris. We're leaving now," Draco bellowed, pulling Sasha by her arm and out of the room. I could hear them arguing but I couldn't make out what they were saying. It wasn't any of my concern anyway. I had more important shit to deal with, like Paris dropping this information on me.

"So is Sasha right, Paris? Is Draco the other man you were sleeping with?"

"Look, I don't have time for this shit. You can go too. I'll see you in the morning at visiting hours. By then I'll know the process of you getting a DNA test done."

"Are you really kicking me out?" I asked, shocked.

"Yes, I need some time alone. This nurse just told you I didn't need to be stressing and clearly you don't give a fuck because you're trying to pick a fight with me."

"I'm sor—" I started, but she cut me off.

"Yeah, yeah, you're sorry. Just go please." I stood there trying to see if she was serious but her expression never changed. I kissed both twins on the head then laid them down in their bassinet. I couldn't believe this was happening.

I left Paris's room and headed toward the elevator. When I was getting off, surprisingly, Sasha was getting back on it.

"What are you still doing here?" I asked.

"When I was leaving I got a call from the nurse that my friend woke up from his coma. I'm about to go upstairs to check on him."

"You're going to check on the married man you were fucking? What if his wife is up there?"

"If she's in the room with him I'll turn around and leave before she sees me."

"I don't think this is a good idea, Sasha. Here you are accusing Draco of having an affair with Paris but you're having one yourself."

"Don't worry about what I'm doing. I'm a big girl. You should be worrying about whose kids those are that you're ready to drop everything and raise."

"Wow, that's what we're on?"

"I'm sorry, I know that was a low blow but my gut is telling me that those are Draco's kids."

"What proof do you have of this?"

"Call it woman's intuition." Sasha shrugged her shoulders then walked away.

I walked to my car and drove to Paris's house. Sasha's words were imbedded in my head. I knew that Paris and Draco had a thing before, but I figured they ended it when I threatened him.

When I made it to Paris's house I took a quick shower and put on a pair of basketball shorts. This was actually the first time that I'd been at her house alone. I couldn't help but start snooping. There was nothing in her bedroom so I made my way to her spare bedroom slash office. There was a file cabinet sitting in the corner. I opened the drawer and started going through her paperwork. I found the lease to her condo and was surprised to see that it was in her and Draco's name. That meant they had been fucking around way longer than I thought. This dumb ass nigga actually had her house in his name. I continued to go through more paperwork and found the title to her car. Draco had bought it for her but signed it over to her. This was why nothing I did ever impressed her. Draco was out here spending real bread on her ass. He was out here acting like he didn't have a wife at home. If Sasha ever found out about this, she would be devastated. I could never be the one to hurt my sister like this. I made sure to put the paperwork back where I found it and left the room. I poured me a drink and sat on the couch. It was all starting to make sense to me. Why Draco was so protective of Paris and why she was so distant from me. If Paris knew what was good for her, she better hope those twins were mine. I literally gave up everything for her ass. Just thinking about this was making my blood boil. It was to the point where I couldn't even lay down to sleep. I tried to call Paris because I had some questions that needed answering but she, of course, didn't answer. I knocked my drink back and closed my eyes until I finally fell asleep a couple hours later. I wasn't going to make any hasty decisions until after I got the DNA test done and the results came back.

Chapter 11
Sasha

I knew it was stupid of me to sneak to Jhayce's room to check on him but at this point, I ain't have shit to lose. I should have listened to my brother but my conscience wouldn't let me leave the hospital until I knew he was okay. I knew that those twins were for Draco because of the way he looked at them. He was in love with those kids. That look further proved what I needed to take everything from his ass.

"You really fucking playing with me, huh Sasha, like I would knock yo' shit back," Draco told me once we were in the hallway. I snatched my arm from him because he was tripping.

"What the fuck did I do? You in there holding her fucking babies like you the fucking father and not my fucking husband," I screamed at him, drawing unwanted attention, but I didn't give a fuck. This nigga had me feeling like I was losing my mind.

"And you the one that was fucking a nigga in the bed that we shared, so make it make sense," he barked at me with his finger in my face. I noticed he didn't even deny what the fuck I'd just said.

"Okay, I did, and apologized for the shit. What the fuck

else do you want me to do Draco?" I asked him, out of fucking answers.

"Sign the fucking divorce papers so I can really be rid of yo' dog ass."

He looked at me like I was trash on the street. I'd never felt so low in my life. At one time I felt like I was the only girl in his world, but I guess there was always room for another. I couldn't believe that he was about to throw our marriage away behind my one mistake when he had made plenty.

"You act like you never cheated on me Draco," I threw out there for good measure.

"Bitch, I never cheated on you once we were married. What the fuck are you talking about?" He backed me into the wall out of view. Draco had never called me out my name, so I knew it was over. He had brought his street life into our marriage so I might as well just sign the papers now. I thought he was about to hit me. His eyes were red with venom as he put his hand against the wall on the side of my face. I put my head down as the tears rolled down my face. I wasn't hurt, because I knew the moment I jumped on another nigga's dick that it was over. For me to get that close to another nigga, my mind had already left Draco. I didn't know what I was holding on for. Maybe it was because I knew the type of man he was and didn't want another woman to experience him the way I did, or I just didn't want him with anyone else. I was selfish. I wanted Draco to myself. That's why I never wanted to give him babies. Then I would have to split my time with kids and the streets. The streets I couldn't control, but I could control if I got pregnant or not.

"What about now, Dray?" I taunted, calling him by the nickname that Paris felt so comfortable calling him. "I know you fucking Paris and those might be your kids, huh?" I asked with a smirk. "Are you the nigga that she fucked before she met my brother?" I asked him, looking in his eyes. He didn't blink. That was a blessing and a curse because I never knew what the fuck he was thinking.

"And if I am fucking Paris and those are my kids, what the fuck are you gonna do about it? Huh? Not a fucking thing because you ain't got no fucking proof. You an entire fucking judge and can't find no fucking proof that your husband is cheating. What about my love language, huh? Do you know mine? I know yours is touch and affection, and have I not been giving you both? You never had to fucking tell me what to do for you and to you because I was in sync with my fucking wife. I knew what she needed even if she didn't, and you still fucking cheated, but for what? Because you thought I wouldn't find out?" he whispered calmly in my face. "I'm a street nigga. I know shit you think I don't know." He backed away from me as my tears flowed down my cheeks. I watched as he pulled a piece of paper and a pen out of his pocket and tried to hand it to me.

"Let's not waste time and get this shit done, Sasha. I don't give a fuck if you want this marriage to work, I don't. I'm over this shit and you should be, so sign this shit and let's get it started. You know I'll take care of you, but seeing as though I have proof of your infidelity, that spousal shit ain't gon' work, so you on your own with that." He chuckled and I wanted to slap him.

"I'm not signing that shit!" I yelled at him, and his hand gripped the front of my neck, pressing on the middle.

"You really want me to shut this bitch down, huh?" he asked me, forcing the papers in my hand, but I refused to take them. I kept my hand and fingers open. Draco didn't scare me but I knew what he was capable of.

"You could set this bitch on fire like you did our bed and I still wouldn't fucking sign them. For better or worse, right? That's what we promised," I told him, and he laughed.

"Through sickness and in health too, right? But if I kill yo' ass would that be considered being fucking sick or dead, bitch?" I saw him go to his back and I knew he was about to pull his gun out. My mind went wild at how he got past the metal detectors with it.

"You can pull that bitch out, but you better use it. We got a lot of witnesses and I could scream loud as fuck. Do you really wanna go that route with me, Dray Dray," I taunted his ass because he knew I was right. I eased away from him and started to walk away.

"Fuck you and those papers, Draco, because I'll never sign them." I gave him the finger as I walked away from him. I could hear him faintly cursing me out, calling me everything but a child of God until I could hear him anymore.

I walked toward the exit but made a detour to the elevators because I wanted to see if Jhayce was okay. I made my way to the ICU unit and the nurse let me in. I made my way to his room but stopped when I got to the door. I looked through the glass door and noticed Jhayce sitting up on the bed eating food. I didn't see his wife anywhere around so I pushed the door open and stepped inside. I closed the door and his head turned my way. A half smile graced his face as I walked closer to the bed, closing the door behind me.

"Jhayce, how are you?" I said, sitting on the bed beside him.

"What the fuck have you gotten me into, Sasha? Why the fuck did we get shot at and I damn near died?" he shot out question after question like this was my fucking fault.

"I didn't get yo' ass into anything! You came yo' ass to my house and fucked me in my bed that I share with my fucking husband, so don't point your finger at me, nigga. It took two and

I didn't fuck myself," I told him, and he stared at me like I had ten heads.

"You think I don't know who the fuck your husband is? I did my homework on that nigga and I must say that I'm impressed. That nigga been knew I was trying to get at you Sasha, so it ain't a coincidence that we were shot at the gas station close to your house. I almost fucking died because of you Sasha," his voice raised, and I was offended.

"You came to my fucking house, I didn't invite you," I told him.

"But you didn't stop my dick from falling inside of you, did you? Stop acting like a fucking child and take ownership for what the fuck we did. Do you know I had to tell my fucking wife what the fuck happened and she was not happy. She threatened to tell my fucking job, which could get both of us fired and our careers in jeopardy," he said, cutting his eyes at me, "My fucking wife went downstairs to get food and will be back up at any moment and you don't need to fucking be here. You have fucked up enough," he said to me, and my heart dropped. That hurt more than the shit Draco did. I was stuck in my seat. I turned to him, looking in his beautiful face. Something about the way he was talking to me turned me on. I didn't give a fuck where we were, but I wanted him.

"You are right, Jhayce, but I couldn't control myself when we were at my house. With you, I lose all control." I stood and was in front of him. My hand rested on his shoulders as his head fell back. I rubbed his neck up and down as we stared in each other's eyes. I knew I was his weakness and he could never resist me. I pulled his hospital gown down and off. He sat on the bed butt ass naked with a hard dick, and my mouth salivated. I had to taste him. I got on my knees and he tried to stop me.

"Sasha, what the fuck you doing?" He put up little resistance as my mouth met the tip of his dick. The precum oozed out and I sucked it off.

"You know what I'm doing, just enjoy the moment before wifey comes back," I told him, and he fell back on his elbows. I took his entire dick in my mouth and bobbed my head up and down in slow motion. My hand massaged his balls, causing a friction that would drive him crazy. He started to fuck my mouth slow and I knew I had him.

"Mmmhhhhh, fuck Sasha, yo' mouth vicious as fuck," he moaned, gripping the back of my head. I felt his dick jump at the back of my throat and knew he was about to nut. He yanked my head up and brought my face to his for a sloppy kiss. I stood and pulled my dress over my ass and mounted him. I felt his head at my opening and didn't give a fuck about using protection. I slid down easy and began to ride him like a cowgirl. Up and down, I rode him and he gripped my waist and hips to control the motion. Before I could nut, I felt myself being yanked off him and dragged to my feet.

"Bitch, you can't get enough, huh? You fucking yo' side nigga in the hospital that I put his bitch ass in." I couldn't gather myself at the revelation that he just gave me. Draco had shot at us at the gas station. "You a nasty bitch and that man's wife right down the hallway." He picked me up like a rag dog and threw me against the wall. I slid down it, out of breath. He stood over me, pulling me to my feet.

"Bitch, you lucky cameras are all around this bitch because I would blow yo' shit back and it'll be fuck the divorce papers because death would do us part. Go clean yo' dirty ass pussy," he barked at me, pushing me into the bathroom.

"What the fuck is going on in here? Aren't you the bitch that was fucking my husband and damn near got him killed? You gotta be a bold bitch to come in here after the shit you did."

I turned to see his wife storming toward me. Draco caught her before she could get to me.

"Ma'am, I understand that you are upset, but we were leaving. Bitch, let's go!" Draco looked at me and I felt like the scum of the earth. I watched as Jhayce's wife moved Draco's hands from around her.

"If you don't get this homewrecking whore out of this room, she'll leave in a body bag," she barked at me, and Draco let her go. Draco looked at me like I disgusted him, but I walked out with my head held high. I didn't give a fuck what none of them thought because I was that bitch and forever would be that bitch.

I walked out the room with Draco on my heels. I was over him and anything he had to say. He wanted our marriage to come to an end and I was about to give him exactly what the fuck he wanted, but I needed answers.

"You about the dizziest bitch I have ever seen in my life. You fucking this nigga in the hospital? You that desperate for a nigga that ain't gon' never leave his wife. You just made a fucking fool of yourself," he barked at me as I damn near ran down the hallway. I didn't want to hear shit he was saying because I had chosen my battle and I was going to fight it alone. I turned to him and he almost ran over me.

"I'll sign your fucking divorce papers because I know I'm damaged goods to you and you have no use for me, but I need to know, are those babies in there yours?" I asked him straight out because I was tired of the cat and mouse game. "Are you really helping that bitch because she was new to the city or is she your side bitch?" I asked him.

"It doesn't matter what the fuck I'm doing with Paris because it is none of your concern. Sign the fucking papers Sasha," he said as we got on the elevator. My life went from sugar to shit in a matter of weeks and I didn't know how to fix it. I didn't want to divorce him but fucking Jhayce and him catching me was something I knew he wouldn't forgive, on top of me getting an abortion. It was what it was. I took the papers and pen from him and signed where I needed to sign because there was no use in trying to explain anything to him. Draco turned into the Incredible Hulk when he was mad so arguing with him would get me nowhere. I handed hm the papers back and he smiled like a Cheshire cat. I leaned against the wall of the elevator and looked at him. The man I once gave my all to was now over and done with me, and I couldn't handle it. I may have signed those divorce papers, but this wasn't the last that he was going to see of me. If my intuition was right, then I knew in my heart that the twins were his and I would make their life hell whether we were married or not. As we walked off the elevator with him walking out before me, he turned in my direction.

"And to answer your question, the twins are mine. I was the nigga she was fucking all along. They have the same birth mark I have," he said, pulling his shirt to the side displaying the dark spot that covered half his shoulder. "So tell your brother he about to get his feelings fucked over for being a cover up because Paris and the twins belong to me," he said before walking away from me, laughing like he'd just told a funny joke.

Chapter 12
Draco

Two weeks had passed since Paris delivered the twins. I'd been with her every single day since then. Jonah was in his feelings since he had to get a DNA test and I'm sure Sasha already told him I said the twins are mine. He came up to the hospital to get the test the day after the babies were born, but he hadn't been around Paris since then. I knew he was nowhere but at Sasha's house with her. They're both most likely having a pity party for each other.

If I'm being honest, I didn't give a fuck about none of that shit. It gave me more time to spend with Paris and my kids. As much as Paris didn't want to admit it, she'd finally come around and said she thinks they're mine. She'd be a damn fool if she thought otherwise. They had her complexion but my features were starting to come through some and they both had my birthmark on their shoulder.

The only thing left was for me to convince Paris to move in with me. The DNA results would be here today and once they showed the twins were mine, I was going to make my move. I didn't have a problem spending the night here with her to help with the twins, but I was ready for my kids to have their own room. I already paid someone to set up the nursery and it's just about done now.

I looked over at Paris breastfeeding our daughter Draya and it was the most beautiful thing I'd ever seen. I'm proud of the way Paris had stepped up to motherhood. I was the one excited about this pregnancy. This was something that she never wanted, but I'm glad she's getting the hang of it. That's one of the main reasons why I didn't want to leave her side. I didn't want her to get overwhelmed or think she's in this alone. I'd heard about the kind of shit that happened when a woman had postpartum depression.

I was ready to tell my mother about the twins because I knew she'd be excited that she was finally a grandmother. I'm just not sure how she's going to take it when she finds out about Paris and my affair. She loved Sasha but I knew she'd never mistreat Paris or my kids. I wanted to let my mother know what was going on when Paris was pregnant, but Paris said wait for the DNA test so that I wouldn't get my mother's hopes up high.

"Take a picture, it'll last longer." Paris smiled as she looked back down at our daughter.

"I can't help but look at you. You're the most beautiful woman in the world to me right now. You gave me two seeds and you're still sexy as hell."

"Thanks, but I don't feel sexy right now. I still feel big as a house. Will you still love me if I don't lose these love handles?"

"You just gave birth two weeks ago so I'm sure you don't have anything to worry about. To answer your question though, yes, I would still love you. I'll make sure to pay more attention to your love handles."

Paris was about to respond when my phone started to ring. I looked down at it and saw that it was Sasha. I had no idea why she was calling because I hadn't heard from her since I left her in the hospital parking lot. I hit ignore only for her to call back again.

"Just answer it, I won't be mad. I don't need your phone waking Drake up or you'll be the one putting him back to sleep," she said, serious.

The last thing I wanted was for him to wake up. I loved my twins to death but when my son was woken up out of his sleep, he's a menace. Now Draya, on the other hand, was calm as hell. As long as she's fed and dry she didn't like to be bothered. I could already tell she's going to be a handful.

My phone rang again and this time I stepped out of the room to answer. I wasn't doing it to hide anything. I was doing it out of courtesy for Paris and my kids. There was no telling what Sasha wanted and I didn't want to disturb them when I cursed her ass out.

"Why the hell do you keep calling my phone?" I answered.

"Damn, that's how you answer the phone for your wife now?"

"Ex-wife," I corrected her.

"No baby, I'm still the wife until we go to court, and don't you forget that while you're over there playing house with your mistress and illegitimate kids."

"Don't you ever address my kids as that. Their names are Draya and Drake," I stated proudly.

"Wow, so you're going to actually disrespect me like that and name those kids after you so that everyone can know about your affair?"

"My kids names don't have shit to do with you or anyone else. I asked you over and over to give me a baby and you didn't want to. Yet you let dude knock you up and you aborted the kid. Now that I have the opportunity to be a father, I'm going to take full advantage of it. They also have my last name already as well," I pointed out. It took some convincing, but I finally had gotten Paris to agree to name the kids after me. If I had my way, my son would have been a junior, but Drake was close enough to my name. Paris was trying to say naming them after me was embarrassing and classless because now everyone would know that I'm the father. I didn't give a fuck what anybody thought though. Those were my seeds and in order for them to continue on with my legacy they needed to have my name. Paris wasn't worried about other people's feelings when she was riding my dick on the regular, so she shouldn't be worried now.

"What the fuck ever, Draco. Your mother called and asked me to go to lunch with her tomorrow. I need to know what I'm telling her."

"Shit, tell her the truth. I'm not hiding anything from her either because I'm going to make sure she's in her grandkids' lives."

"What's the truth? That you left me for some young ass bitch that you got pregnant?"

"Yep, make sure not to leave out the part about you fucking a nigga in our crib and me catching you riding his dick in the hospital. As a matter of fact, don't worry about it. I'm going to see her today after the DNA results," I told her before hanging up the phone.

Sasha had some motherfucking nerves to act like she was in her feelings. She was either the boldest or dumbest bitch I knew. She was acting all distraught every time I brought up the word divorce only for her to jump on that nigga's dick again the first chance she got. She better be lucky we were in the hospital that day or I would have finished what I started at the gas station. If it wasn't for the cameras, I would have allowed dude's wife to beat her ass. That's how I knew my marriage was really over because had that been a couple years back, I would have knocked Sasha's head through the wall if I saw her riding another man's dick. She was doing all that like she wasn't begging me to suck my dick a few days before that. I guess since I wasn't supplying the dick to her anymore, she was desperate. If I wasn't trying to do right by Paris and raise a family with her, I would have dicked old dude's wife down right there in that hospital room in front of his ass just for playing with my top. She was a bad little bitch and it showed that dude had a type. I'd pipe his wife down though, and she'd forget about his cripple ass being laid up in that hospital.

By the time I finished my phone call, Paris was in the bed with the twins sleep. I wasn't sleepy so I decided to clean up for her and order us something to eat. I wasn't in the mood to cook, and I wanted to lighten Paris's load. Once I finished straightening up the Dasher was outside with our order. Since I was already down there, I decided to check Paris's mail. My heart almost leaped out of my chest when I saw the letter we were waiting on was finally here. I ran back up the stairs and placed everything on the table. I was now mad as hell that Paris was sleep. I wanted to wake her up but I knew she'd curse me out. That's where my son got that cranky shit from. I picked the letter up but then put it back down. I didn't want to open her mail up without her consent and this was something that we needed to do together.

The hour that Paris remained sleep felt like an eternity. I was happy as hell when her phone started ringing or she would have still been sleep. She looked down at her phone and declined the call before climbing out of bed and stepping out of the room. I was on her heels literally as we made our way to the living room.

"That was Jonah calling. I guess the results came back," Paris said.

"They did, I took your copy from the mailbox but I didn't

want to open it without you," I informed her, handing her the letter.

Paris took the letter from me and opened it. I didn't know why my confidence was starting to fade all of a sudden. During her entire pregnancy I claimed the twins were mine and there was never a doubt, so now with the proof in front of us I was holding my breath.

"Well, congratulations Draco, this says that there's a 0% chance that Jonah is the father," she said solemnly.

"That's good news. Why the fuck you sitting there like a sick puppy?"

"Because this shit is fucked up, Draco. You're still a married man. What are we going to tell our kids when they grow up?"

"We're going to tell them that they were made out of love, and I won't be married for long. I told you I filed the divorce papers and I already told Sasha the twins are mine."

I know it was fucked up the way I told Sasha, but her ass was asking for it that day. She kept asking and I was tired of lying. I had said once my kids were born I would never hide or deny them. I didn't even have any intentions on telling her that day or that way but after she disrespected me by fucking that nigga again, all my respect for her went out the window. At that point there was no need for me to sugar coat the situation.

"Yeah, I hear you Draco."

"I'm serious Paris, they already have my name. They never have to know I was married when we started dealing with each other. It's not like they'll be asking questions anytime soon." I shrugged.

"I guess so. There's nothing we can do about it now."

"Nope, now I can finally tell my OG. She's going to be happy as hell. She thought she'd never see the day."

"What if she tries to treat them different because of Sasha?"

"She's not like that, baby. You don't have anything to worry about."

Paris and I talked a little longer before we finally sat down to eat. We were halfway through our meal when someone started banging on the door like the police.

"Bitch, open the door. I know you're in there," Jonah yelled as he continued banging on the door. I didn't want him to wake the kids so I rushed to open the door.

"Aye, gone somewhere with that shit. You got the test results so there's nothing here for you. Paris is mine and so are the twins, so you can beat your feet."

"Fuck you Draco, I knew y'all two was fucking. I should have told my sister when I first confronted your ass about this. I can't believe I betrayed my sister because I was scared I would lose this ho," Jonah yelled.

"Nigga, who the fuck you calling a ho?" Paris yelled back.

"You, bitch, only a ho would fuck a married man and his brother-in-law, then you tried to pin them fucking kids on me. What were you going to do if Draco and Sasha decided to work on their marriage? We were just going to be one big happy family? Huh bitch? You hear me—" was the last word Jonah got out before I knocked him in his shit. I didn't tolerate disrespect and he had called Paris one too many bitches. I get that he's mad but he brought this on himself. If he was so sure that me and her were fucking, I didn't know why he pursued her to begin with. I tried to warn his simple ass.

"Watch your motherfucking mouth. Don't come in here with all that shit. My kids in the room sleep." I added more salt to his wound.

That must've really hit a nerve because he jumped up and charged toward me, but he was no match for me. I jumped out the way and he went tumbling back to the floor.

"Yo, Jonah, you need to go. I'm not about to talk to you while you're like this," Paris informed him.

"Bet, I'll go now, but you best believe this ain't the last of you seeing me, Paris. I'll be back to get my shit another day," he said, and I didn't like the way that sounded.

"I hope that's not a threat because I'd hate to have to turn you into worm food," I warned him.

"You ain't the only one with a gun. Just remember that," he said before walking out.

"Yo, that nigga got some screws loose. I'm not comfortable with you living here. He can easily get in here. You and the kids need to move in with me," I told Paris.

"What? No, Draco, holler at me when your divorce is finalized."

"Come on, Paris, this has to do with you and the safety of my kids. Hell, you can move into my condo and I'll move into this one. No one knows where that one is, so y'all will be safe."

"You're tripping, Dray. Jonah isn't like that, but I'll think about your offer only because you have more space," Paris said before walking away to go check on the twins. If I knew our world was going to flipped upside down from this day forward, I would have dragged Paris out of her house and to mine.

Chapter 13
Jonah

Paris had me fucked up if she thought she was about to get away with fucking over me. Sasha could handle shit the way she saw fit, but I had to put a plan in motion. Paris couldn't just go around fucking over people's heart like it was trash, and she was about to feel me. I laughed to myself at the fucking stunt Draco and Paris pulled back at her condo, but I would have the last laugh. I spent more time with that bitch during her pregnancy than Draco did. That nigga was playing with my sister's feelings, had her thinking their marriage was on the right track when it wasn't. There's a special place in hell for niggas like him.

As I drove the highway back to Sasha's house I let the voice of Kevin Gates take over my mind.

That lil' pussy got some power in it
That lil' pussy got some power in it
Super soaker, need a towel for it
Drippin' on me like a showerhead
Throw it back and arch your back when you doin' me
Bustin' back to back to back when you doin' me

I be runnin' back to get it back when I'm through
Lotta Birkin bags, back to back
Got the black and the white and the blue
That lil' pussy doin' somethin' to me
Ooh, that lil' pussy feel good to me
You know what you got and girl, you got a lot
Skeet from the back and I just wanna watch
Climb up on top and ride me like a bike
You got that power, power
Tryna beat it for hour, hours
If it's yours, it's mine, it's ours

The lyrics described every emotion that I felt. Paris was a sweet woman but her pussy had power over me. I wanted to lock her ass in a cage and only let her out when I wanted some pussy or to take care of the twins. Paris was the type of woman that you had no choice but to give everything you had to give to her because she was a charmer. I saw how she got Draco wrapped around her finger. She's beautiful, educated, and had spunk that would drive a real nigga insane. That's just what she did to me. To watch Draco and Paris together ate at my soul because that was supposed to be me with her and my babies she was caring for. Instead, I got the short end of the stick and a broken heart. I pushed my Camaro to 120 as I made the exit to Sasha's house. I would run everything down to her, get her opinion, and tell her my plan. If she wasn't fucking with it then I'd make my moves solo. I didn't need help anyway. I got out the car in front of Sasha's apartment since Draco had the fucking locks changed. He didn't think I knew about him burning their bed, but Sasha kept nothing from me. I wanted to knock that nigga's shit back but Sasha said that she would handle it.

I walked into the house and found Sasha sitting on the

couch with depressing ass music playing. She had a wine glass in her hand and on the table was a bottle of Cole Signature Merlot. In fact, there were three bottles, of which two were empty so she was working on the third. I shook my head because Draco had really done a number on her and I didn't like this shit. Sasha was a strong and independent woman, and now she was a shell of that or even less than that. I walked in closer as she sipped from her glass and stood over her.

"What the fuck happened since I left? You weren't like this before," I asked her, and her bloodshot eyes met mine and I could tell she'd been crying.

"I called Draco." She sniffed and tears poured from her eyes. "He is going to fucking divorce me for that young bitch that he's living with! What the fuck am I supposed to do? He changed the fucking locks and everything I own was in that house and now I can't get it! He got my laptop, clothes, just shit I need to go to work. What the fuck am I supposed to do?!" she yelled, but I knew it wasn't intentional. She was upset and had every right to be. I sat down next to her, leaning to the back of the couch.

"You gon' get yo' shit back, sis, and I'm going to get it," I told her, and she gave me a weird look.

"Jonah, did you take your medicine? If you didn't, I'll call Mommy and have her come get you." She sat her glass down on the table and stared at me hard.

She knew I hated when she treated me like an invalid. That's the main reason that I left Washington, because I was tired of my parents treating me like I couldn't take care of myself. Sasha was no different, but I hadn't planned on staying in her domain like the current shit I'm in.

"You got that look in your eyes, Jonah. How long has it been, and don't fucking lie to me?" she gritted, and I rolled my eyes. She knew I couldn't lie to her and even if I did, she would know. I couldn't get shit past her. I guess I was taking too long because she did a sprint from the sofa to the room I slept in and started going through my things. I ran behind her because I knew what she was up to. When I got there she was going through my bags, pulling my clothes out. When she didn't find what she was looking for, she went to the dresser and started to pull my shit out, and that's when I stopped her. I knew what she was looking for but she would never find it.

"Fuckin' stop, you ain't gon' find that shit!" I yelled at her, yanking her back.

"Why the fuck you not taking your medicine, Jonah?! It ain't safe when you don't take that shit. I'm calling Momma," she yelled in my face and tried to run away from me, but I yanked her by the neck.

"It's just been two weeks, calm down. I feel good so I don't need that shit, sis, and you know it. They put me on medication to hinder me from reality, but I'm not taking that shit. I am going to embrace it," I told her, because that's how I felt.

When we were growing up my mother said I would have these psychosis spells where I would sit in my room, all lights off, not eating or using the bathroom for weeks. Then after that phase I would go to school and find the smallest rodent, whether it be a roach or a rat, and torture it. It had gotten so bad that we had a project to do my senior year in high school. We had to pick an animal to analyze it. Pick the organs and label them. I found a stray cat around the house and did my own version of labeling it. I brought the cat to school and dismembered every part of it in front of the class. My mother was called and I had to be homeschooled for the remainder of the year. I didn't understand it until she took me to a psychiatrist, and I was diagnosed with bipolar schizophrenia. The doctor stated that I had a fixation on animals because they were the weakest and if it wasn't fixed with the proper medication, it could lead me to kill people. I would never hurt a soul. For once I wanted to feel regular and not like a fucking zombie.

"You need your medicine, Jonah. I saw how you were looking at Paris when she had the babies, and I know you must feel a type of way. Talk to me Jonah, please. Draco is a different type of monster and you don't want that type of smoke. I need you levelheaded," she pleaded with me, but I didn't understand it. Yes, I was crushed and wanted to fuck something up, but my mind wouldn't let me. I had some other shit in mind. Now that Sasha was on my ass, I would carry out my plan solo. I didn't give a fuck what kinda fucking Freddy Krueger this nigga was, but he was about to see me as Michael Myers.

"I just want to feel human, Sasha. I walked around like a zombie for the past ten years and now I have control of my feelings and emotions. I won't go back down that dark road," I promised her and grabbed her hand. I led her back to the living room, and we sat on the sofa. I got up to get another glass of wine to drink with her. I needed something stronger, but the wine would do. It had a sweet taste and I liked it. After we finished the bottle, Sasha was hanging on by a thread. She eventually fell asleep on the couch. I carried her to her bedroom to lay her down. I threw the sheet over her and left the room.

I went back to my room and picked up my shit that she threw everywhere. I dressed in all back down to my boots and grabbed my keys and phone off the table nearby. I got in my ride and headed straight to my destination. After about thirty minutes of riding, I shut my lights off as I parked my car on the side street where Paris lived. I didn't know their living situation but I knew Draco wasn't there because I had been scoping the condo out for the past week. He always left late at night but was there before the sun came out. Now was the perfect time for me to execute my plan. I got out the car, making sure to put my black gloves on each hand. I crept up the side of the building and went in through the side door. I still had a key to her condo, and I knew she didn't change the locks. I slowly unlocked the door and slid in. I walked through the living room but stopped in my tracks when I heard Paris singing to the twins.

> *Last night I prayed on a fallen star*
> *That you never have a broken heart*
> *Though the world is cold, just remember who you are*
> *And I pray that you never have a rainy day*
> *And no matter what people say*
> *Even when it hurts it'll be okay*

I didn't know if it was some shit she made up or an actual song, but the conviction in her voice was heartfelt. She loved her babies and it made me even more angry. I thought about backing away and leaving well enough alone, but my feet wouldn't move. I came here for a reason so I couldn't back out now. I walked further into the condo to her room. I pushed the door open slowly and quietly and stood there. I watched as she held both babies singing to them. She never noticed me. I waited until she put the babies to bed to step in the room. I closed the door and she jumped.

"Draco, you could let me know when you come in the house, boy. Yo' ass always quiet as a damn church mouse," she said as she started to turn around. The fact that she said that nigga's name infuriated me more. In one swift motion, I grabbed her into a chokehold before she could see my face. I put the wet cloth over her nose to make her pass out. She fought until she couldn't fight anymore and her body went limp. I carried her to the car then came back to lift the twins and a bag of what they needed and left the house. Draco gon' be in for a rude awakening when he returned and saw his pretty little family wasn't intact the way he left it. The Boogeyman had officially come out of retirement and Jigsaw was back to play for a little while.

Chapter 14
Paris

I woke up in a bed that didn't belong to me. I looked around the dark room, confused. My memory was currently foggy. I remember putting the twins down for bed and then someone entering my bedroom. I thought it was Draco but being that I was knocked out, I now knew it wasn't him. The person didn't make a sound and I couldn't make out their face. This shit was so fucked up on so many levels.

My ass should have listened to Draco when he told me to move into his condo with him. The thing was, I didn't like to feel like I was being controlled, so at times I didn't think rationally. Now not only did I put my life in danger but my kids as well.

I turned on the lamp that was on the end table then I stood from the bed so I could see if there were any clues to where I was. I immediately had to sit back down though because I was dizzy as hell. I don't know what the hell was going on with me. I took a deep breath then stood up again. This time I felt a little better. I didn't have time to dwell on how I was feeling. I needed to find out where my kids were.

I went to go look out the window but it had bars on them

and the window was boarded up. I didn't know how long I'd been out, but I didn't think it was that long that someone was able to set this shit up. That meant it's someone I knew and this was on purpose. The first person that came to mind was Sasha. This bitch was in her feelings and had someone kidnap me.

I walked over to the door and attempted to turn the knob but it wouldn't budge. Someone had actually locked me up in a room. This was shit that I read about or saw on TV. I never imagined I would experience this is real life. To be honest, I didn't think people actually did this shit.

I banged on the door to see if I could get someone's attention.

"Let me out of here right now. Where's my kids?" I yelled. There was no answer so I continued to beat on the door for what felt like almost an hour until I heard someone walking toward the door. I looked around the room to see what I could use to knock the person upside their head. The only thing I could find was a book on the dresser, so that would have to do. It was either that or the lamp. If I used the lamp then I would be stuck in darkness.

When the door was pushed open I reached out to swing but stopped when I saw who it was.

"What the fuck is going on? You helped your sister kidnap me?" I asked Jonah.

He looked at me before giving me a sinister laugh. It was something about him that was different. The look in his eyes made me take a step back. It was as if his eyes were hollow and he was missing his soul.

"Do you think my sister would jeopardize her career for you and Draco's bitch ass? This is all me. You tried to play me Paris, and now it's time for me to show you who I really am. All I wanted was for you to love me the way I loved you, but instead you chose to continue to fuck Draco behind my back. I mean, who the fuck does that? What does he have that I don't besides a wife?" Jonah bellowed.

"It wasn't like that, Jonah. I never meant to hurt you. I really did care about you," I admitted.

"If lying to me the entire time that we were together is your way of showing me you care, you're a more fucked up individual than I thought," he replied.

"Says the person that kidnaps a woman and her kids. I should have listened to Draco. You're fucking crazy," I said without thinking, and before I knew it Jonah reached out and slapped the shit out of me. I almost lost my balance, but I caught myself.

"Don't ever call me that again, and I never want to hear you mention that nigga's name again. You're my woman now and those are my twins. We're going to be a family like I discussed. You live here now, so get comfortable," he stated as he turned to leave the room.

This motherfucker was actually a psycho. When Draco told me that Jonah was crazy, I thought he was just on some hating shit because he didn't want me to be with anyone other than him. I didn't think this man was actually crazy, like he needed to be locked up in the psych ward crazy. He never showed me any indication that something was wrong with him. He was always attentive, loving, and caring to me. I didn't know what changed for him to all of a sudden show this side of himself. It was as if this side had been suppressed. I knew it had to be more than him finding out the twins weren't his, because he wasn't this bad when I asked for the DNA test.

"Wait, don't lock me up in here. Where are my kids?" I asked, getting his attention.

"Our kids are in their room. Once I know that you can behave, I'll allow you out to see them."

"So they're supposed to starve to death? I am the source of their food."

"Of course not, there's a breast pump inside of the drawer over there with some bottles. I would never allow anything to happen to JJ or Johana." He smiled.

I looked at him confused as hell because I didn't know who the fuck those people were. His ass was apparently losing it right before my eyes.

"Huh? Who the hell is that? That's not my kids' names," I finally said.

"It is their names. From now on they will be addressed as JJ and Johana. If you didn't catch on, that's Jonah Junior and Johana is our princess. We can't have them growing up with another man's name. We don't want them confused, now do we?" he asked with conviction in his voice.

I was ready to go off on him but out of fear of him smacking me again, I played along for the sake of me and my kids making it out of this alive.

"Okay, you're right Jonah, anything you say baby. I promise to behave, I just want to spend some time with my kids. Please allow me to feed them on my own. They need the connection to their mother."

He looked at me as if he was thinking about what I said. I closed my eyes and prayed to God that he agreed. I knew he said that he would never hurt the kids, but at the rate he was going he could snap out any minute and snap all of our necks. I knew by now Draco had been to the house and noticed that we were gone. I just needed to hold out until he figured out where we were. With his resources and skills, it shouldn't be hard unless Jonah had taken us across state lines, then it'd be up to me to get us to safety.

"Okay, I'll bring them in here to you when they wake up. I don't trust you not to try and escape yet, so you won't be leaving this room yet. The minute you do something that I don't approve of, I won't allow you to see them for a week. Do you understand?"

I nodded my head up and down because I was at a loss for words. I couldn't believe that he was serious. The man that I shared a bed with damn near every night was a stranger to me. I didn't know how I could be so dumb. No, I wasn't dumb, because he didn't show any signs. Hell, the only argument we had was when I told him I didn't want to move in with him. Even still, instead of him going overboard he left the house to calm down.

Jonah made his way out of the room and this time I didn't stop him. I went and sat down on the bed. All I wanted to do was ball up and cry, but I couldn't do that. I needed to be strong for my kids. I needed to show Jonah that he couldn't break me. I needed to use my brain to figure this shit out, and I needed to preserve my energy.

A couple hours passed when Jonah came in the room with the twins. He kept his word and brought them so I could feed them. Once I finished feeding and burping them, he reached out to take them from my arms.

"No, please don't, I just want to spend time with them," I pleaded with tears in my eyes. Fuck being strong right now. I was a mother feeling detached from her babies. I might not have wanted kids, but that didn't stop my maternal instinct of loving them more than life itself.

"You get one hour and one hour only. They need to learn how to sleep in their own bed so that they won't grow up to be spoiled brats," he told me before storming out of the room.

I didn't give a fuck what he was talking about. These were my kids and they were the only ones I would ever have, so if they grew up to be spoiled then I was fine with that. They deserved to have the world handed to them.

I held both of my kids and smiled down at them as I sang lullaby after lullaby. If they couldn't sleep with me I wanted my face to at least be the last face they saw before they went to sleep.

"Mommy is so sorry that this happened. I love you two so damn much. Daddy is going to come find us and if he doesn't, then I'll figure something out," I whispered, making sure that Jonah couldn't overhear me and spazz again.

He came back in the room exactly an hour later. I knew this because the crazy fucker had a big ass timer on the wall. He actually thought this shit through. I wondered how long it took him to come up with this plan and execute it. It had to have been longer than today, well, last night because it's after midnight so it's a new day. It was as if this was his plan B all along if anything ever went wrong between us.

"Here's a bottle of water. I know you don't eat this late at night. The dresser has clothes in it for you and that door over to your left is a bathroom. Before you get any crazy ideas, there are no windows in there so you can't escape me."

"As if I'd try to escape without my kids," I pointed out.

"That reason alone is why you will never have them for a long period of time alone. As long as they're not in here with you or I have one of them, you will never try to leave me."

"I'm sorry, but I have to ask. What do you plan on accomplishing from this? Do you think it's going to make me love you? Holding me against my will is only going to make me hate you."

"Love and hate, I don't see the difference. Either or, I'm still on your mind and you won't be with that nigga," he laughed.

"Draco will—" I started but stopped when I felt Jonah pop in my mouth. I mean, I could actually taste the blood in my mouth. I had never had a man put his hands on me in this way. I might have gotten choked up a little, but it was never geared to actually hurt me. It was usually me out of pocket and them trying to calm me down.

"Didn't I tell you not to mention that nigga's name in my presence? I meant that shit. I don't want to hurt you Paris, but I will punish you if you're disobedient," he said before walking out of the room, slamming the door behind him.

I rushed to the bathroom so I could try to rinse my mouth out before it swelled up. I looked around the bathroom and it had all the products that I used down to the razors. It was as if he never planned on me leaving this house for real. I rinsed my mouth out then went back in the room to see what clothes he had for me. I looked in the drawers that were filled to the brim with clothes. Tears filled my eyes as I pulled out a pair of leggings, a t-shirt, and panties. I went back in the bathroom and climbed in the shower. As the water hit my body the dam broke. I could no longer hold in the tears that needed to escape. I cried for a good thirty minutes before I finally calmed down. I finished up my shower, moisturized my body, then got dressed. I was exhausted and all I wanted to do was get some sleep and forget this nightmare. That idea was short lived though, because when I exited the bathroom Jonah was laying in the bed. I just knew he didn't plan on me sleeping in the same bed as him.

"What are you doing in my bed, Jonah?"

"Shut the fuck up and come lay down. It's not like we haven't slept in the same bed together before."

I debated on whether I should protest or not. He'd already hit me in my mouth twice for mentioning Draco's name, so there was no telling what he was capable of if I kept going against what he said. I guess I wasn't moving fast enough for him because in one swift motion, he pulled me by my arm and yanked me into bed with him.

"In case you haven't noticed, I make the rules in here. You

do what I say and this process could go a lot easier. You're forcing my hand right now and testing my patience. Now close your eyes and take your ass to sleep. You're going to need your energy for when our kids wake up."

I didn't even say anything else to Jonah. There was no response I could say that wouldn't make him knock my teeth out next time, so instead I laid there staring at the wall for what felt like hours until I finally fell asleep.

Chapter 15
Draco

I had to be losing my fucking mind. Something in my gut told me to turn around and go check on Paris and the twins but against my better judgement, I went ahead and handled my business. I had to make sure that the 18 wheeler carrying the guns went to its respectful place. That and the shipment of pure heroine got to my warehouse to be broken down. That took a little over two hours before I headed back to Paris's condo.

When I pulled up, shit felt off. I couldn't quite put my finger on it, but I knew something had happened before I even got on the elevator. Soon as I got off and walked to her door, I noticed it was slightly ajar. Trying my fucking best not to panic, I went in and could have set this bitch on fire. There were clothes thrown everywhere. It was a fucking disaster. I walked around the condo yelling for Paris but she never answered. I walked in the room and didn't see her, but the scene looked like she had packed up what she could for her and the kids and left.

My mind was fucked up because when I left, she was good. I noticed her phone on the bed and picked it up. I scrolled through her call log and noticed Jonah calling back to back. That's when it clicked. I knew that nigga wasn't trying to die for fucking with them. Paris wouldn't let him take her and my fucking kids. I mulled over every thought in my head. From her ghosting me to him kidnapping them. I went for the latter because I knew she wasn't fucking with that nigga like that. I took her phone with me and left out the door to go to my gun warehouse, but I had to make a detour first.

I pulled up to where Sasha was living. She didn't know that I knew where she lived but I did. I couldn't trust that bitch so I had eyes on her and Jonah everywhere they went. Sasha didn't move around too much so I knew she was in there. I got out my car and walked to her front door. I picked the lock with my mini screwdriver and let myself in. I walked through her shit quiet as hell and didn't see her. I walked in the hallway to the first door and looked inside. That must've was Jonah's room because men's shit was everywhere. I went to the second room and I opened the door wide and noticed Sasha laid out on the bed snoring. I saw the empty wine bottle on the side of the bed and laughed. I walked closer to the bed and watched her sleep.

Sasha never felt me standing over her. I could have killed her ass just then, but I needed answers that only she could provide. I bent down, grabbing her by the collar of her shirt, yanking her out her slumber. The look on her face was price-less. Crust in her eyes, hair all over her head, ole girl was going through it and I didn't give one fuck.

"What the fuck!? Draco, what the fuck are you doing here? How the fuck did you get in my house?" she barely got out because I was choking the life out of her. I pulled my gun from my waist and put it to her neck.

"Where the fuck did Jonah take Paris and my fucking kids, Sasha?" I gritted, pushing the gun further into her throat. I was gon' off this bitch if she didn't answer me.

"What are you talking about, Draco? Jonah was here before I passed out. He don't give a fuck 'bout Paris or those kids. You need to be trying to make our marriage work instead of worrying about what the fuck they doing," she screamed in my face, and I smacked fire from her fucking mouth with the butt of my gun. I didn't hit her too hard because I prided myself on not putting my hands on women, but she was pushing it.

"Bitch, you know what the fuck I'm talking about! Yo' bitch ass brother took them and you gon' tell me where they are or I'mma start breaking yo' fingers one by one," I barked in her face before pushing her on the bed hard. I sat on top of her and grabbed her hand, starting with her thumb.

"Wait, wait! Draco, I swear I don't know what the fuck Jonah did. I remember him coming in here and us talking and drinking. I don't even remember him putting me in the bed," she said with a shaky voice. I believed her because her eyes never left mine, but she knew something because that was her brother. There was no way she didn't.

"You lying bitch!" I bent her thumb out of place and she screamed. I put my gun in her mouth to silence her.

"Scream again, bitch, and this hallow point gon' be down yo' throat," I told her, and she cried. I didn't give a fuck about her tears because my mind was going crazy and she was wasting fucking time. I bent back her index finger and she took the pain like a champ. I pulled my gun from her mouth.

"I swear, Draco, I don't know what the fuck Jonah's into, but he does suffer from bipolar schizophrenia and he hasn't been taking his meds," she yelped out. Jonah was really fucking crazy and she hooked this nigga up with Paris.

"Fuuuucccckkk! This shit is all my fault! If I would have been honest from the fucking beginning, Paris wouldn't be in this shit show with me." I was mad as fuck because this shit was on me, and now she and my fucking kids were in danger because of my indiscretions. I looked at Sasha and she cried like a choking cat.

"You really love her, huh?" she asked out of the blue. I didn't want to hurt her with a lie so the truth was gon' come out my mouth.

"I love you, but I'm in love with her. Before I even met Paris, I was trying to compromise in our marriage but when it came to kids, you never compromised. It was a no for you. You gave your all to work instead of pouring it into me. I fell in love with Paris before she even got pregnant," I told her the truth because there was no use in lying about it in this moment.

"Wow. I never thought you would fall out of love with me," she tried to ease out.

"I fell out of love with you when I realized you were in love with being a judge. Then you get pregnant for yo' side nigga and aborted it," I told her and continued, "That shit fucked with me more than you fucking that nigga in our bed." I felt myself getting angry all over again.

"Man, fuck all that soft shit. You wasting fucking time because yo' delusional ass brother done kidnapped my family. Either you tell me where they are or I'm out this bitch," I told her, sticking to the task at hand. She looked up at me with hurt and sorrow in her eyes, but I didn't give a fuck.

"Jonah has a house that he thought I didn't know about. I knew he was off his rocker so I had a PI following him for the past month. I can give you the address if you let me up please," she begged, and I got off her but my gun was still on her. I watched as she went to her purse and pulled out a piece of paper. Her trembling hands gave me the paper and I yanked it from her. "Draco, please don't kill my brother. It'll break my parents' heart," she told me with a straight face.

"You think I give a fuck about how your parents feel? I am

going to kill that nigga for fucking with me. I ain't sparing nobody's fucking feelings. Do you think Jonah's sparing my fucking family?!" I barked at her.

"He is sick, Draco. Jonah is not in his right mind," she tried to reason with me, but I wasn't hearing that shit. I was gon' do what I felt was necessary, and that was kill his bitch ass.

"I'm sicker than him. He fucked with the wrong one," I told her and walked out the door just like I walked in. I hopped back in my car and headed to my next destination. I pulled up to my gun warehouse to switch out my guns. I couldn't use my original handgun because that was my baby. My adrenaline was on a million because I didn't know what the fuck Jonah was capable of. If so much as a hair was out of place on them, it was lights out for that nigga. He gon' wish he had killed himself.

"What's up boss, you just left. I told you we could handle the shipment," one of my hittas said, smiling at me when I walked in the door.

"Nah, I know y'all niggas ain't crazy, but I got a situation," I told him, and he looked at me. Before I could finish, this nigga put on his bulletproof vest and grabbed a handgun and a chopper with the drum.

"Who the fuck we gotta kill, Boss?" he asked, ready for war.

"Nah, this on some personal shit. I need two handguns and fuck a vest, because that nigga ain't making that much noise," I told him. My niggas were loyal and ready for whatever, and that's why I fucked with them hard.

Jonah had to know I was going to find him. Threatening Sasha was icing on the cake, and I loved sweets. I was gon' torture that motherfucker for testing my patience.

"Then again, I might need y'all two with me. Y'all just be on standby just in case this nigga act crazy," I told them, and they nodded their heads. I took two of my strongest muscles and we headed to the black-on-black Suburban. If Jonah thought he was getting away alive from this shit, he had another thing coming.

Chapter 16
Paris

It'd been almost a week and a half since I'd been locked up in this room. I didn't know what the hell was taking Draco so long to find us, but I didn't know how much more of this I could take. Jonah had beat my ass every chance he'd had since I'd been here because I wouldn't let him fuck. Just the thought of him touching me made me weak to the stomach.

He kept his word though and allowed me to spend time with the twins. Whenever it's time for me to feed them he allowed them to stay with me for an hour and then after that he took them away. I still wasn't sure if he was working alone or not. I couldn't hear shit through these walls. The most I saw him was at night when he was making me sleep in the same bed with him. I made sure to scrub my body when I woke up in the morning because he held me tight as hell as if I was going to run away while he was asleep. I'd thought about it, but there's a code to the bedroom door and I didn't know it. If I tried to break the door down he'd hear it, and there's no telling what he would do to me then.

I looked down at my watch and saw that it was almost 6:00

P.M. That meant Jonah should be bringing my kids in for me to spend time with them. This was by far the highlight of my day. I was like a kid in the candy store when it came to spending time with my babies. This situation had made me realize how much I loved being a mother to my twins.

I sat for what seemed like an eternity when six o'clock came and went. He was never late with bringing them to see me, and I had them on a set routine, so this was making me nervous. I thought maybe he stepped out to take care of something, but then that would mean he had someone helping him because if not, who the hell was looking out for my babies? They couldn't change themselves. By the time 6:30 came around I couldn't take it anymore, so I climbed out of the bed and started banging on the door. It took about ten minutes before Jonah walked in the room, closing the door behind him. I couldn't help but notice that he was emptyhanded, which was a red flag seeing as this was the time I'm supposed to bond with my kids.

"What the fuck did I tell you about banging on the door like that?" Jonah yelled.

"I'm sorry, but it's like 6:40 and my kids need to eat."

"They are already," he replied.

"What the hell do you mean they are already?" I asked, confused.

"It means exactly what I said. There's going to be some changes around here. Since you've been disobedient to me, it's time to put my foot down. From now on I will give the twins formula until their mother knows how to act, and as long as they have formula then they don't need you."

My heart dropped hearing those words because seeing my kids was the only thing keeping me strong.

"Why are you doing this, Jonah? I've done everything you asked me to do. You promised you would allow me to see my kids at their feeding times."

"Yeah, but if you're not keeping your end of the deal, then why should I?"

"What have I not done that you've asked me to do?" I quizzed.

"I think you know what I want Paris, and you're being difficult."

"Jonah, the kids are barely a month old. I can't have sex right now."

"Cut the bullshit, Paris. You're not bleeding anymore, and I bet if that bitch ass nigga Draco wanted to bust a nut you'd let him. Speaking of him, do you think he's out looking for you, or is he deep in somebody else's pussy by now. It has been a month since y'all fucked. Maybe he went back home to Sasha and she's riding his dick right now while you and his kids are missing," he taunted me.

I tried my best not to let Jonah's words get to me, but I couldn't help but have doubts in the back of my mind because for the life of me, I didn't get why it's taking him so long to find me. I also knew how much Draco loved sex. Was he distraught enough that sex wasn't on his mind, or was he back fucking with Sasha or Alana? I knew both of those bitches would love to rub this shit in my face. I shook my head to make those thoughts leave as quick as they came because as much as it would hurt if that was the case, I couldn't dwell on it. It's time for me to use my instincts of fight or flight. I had to do what I had to do in order for him to let me up out of this room. That's the only way I could check out my surroundings and figure out a way to get up out of this jam.

"Okay, you're right. I'll make a deal with you. I'll give you some pussy, but you have to let me up out of this room. Just looking at these four walls are driving me crazy. I'm not going to run because it's obvious you're the one that loves me and not

Dr—" I started but stopped because I didn't want him to get angry at hearing Draco's name.

"I'm glad you finally got that through your pretty little head. He's nothing but a liar and a cheater. He can never be a good enough for you, baby. Go get yourself together and I'm just going to make sure the twins are good then I'll be back. If you keep your end of the deal then I'll let you out of the room today," he assured me with a smile before walking out of the room.

I walked in the bathroom and took a deep breath as I looked at myself in the mirror. I could barely recognize myself. My eyes were swollen from not sleeping and crying damn near every night. I'd never cried so much in my entire life. My lips were slightly swollen as well but that came from Jonah hitting me in my mouth. There were also bruises on my arms from when he'd snatch me up or push me down. I was really in this bitch looking like a human punching bag. If I got out of this shit, I was definitely making some changes in my life because I refused to ever end up in a situation like this again. If I had to get my kids and leave Atlanta for good, I would.

I washed and brushed my teeth then climbed in and took a quick shower. Just like all the other times, as soon as the water touched my back I broke down crying. It was like the water was my source of therapy. I couldn't believe I had to actually fuck this nigga to see my kids. I didn't know if I'd ever be able to trust a man again after all of this. Hell, I didn't even know if I wanted to trust someone with my heart again. I knew what I did was wrong by not telling Jonah about Draco in the beginning, but even this was to an extreme. I would have rather Jonah had got mad and beat my ass or something than kidnap me. He got me ready to beat Sasha's ass when I got out of here because I felt like she set me up. She knew her brother was a fucking psycho and she introduced us. I was starting to think she wanted me with Jonah because she didn't want me fucking with Draco. I guess she didn't realize the bond and connection me and her husband had because if she did, she would have been left him alone. The nigga been in love with this pussy since the first day I gave him a taste of it.

"Paris, hurry up in there. We don't need the twins waking up disturbing us," Jonah yelled, pulling me from my thoughts as he knocked on the door.

"Okay, give me five minutes," I called out. I hurriedly finished my shower then dried off. I rubbed baby oil on me since I didn't have time to do my full skin care routine. I brushed my hair back into a ponytail then took another deep breath. Never in my life had I ever fucked a man that I didn't want to. I was never forced into sex before. He had me feeling like a prostitute. I wasn't even in the mood for sex so I hoped my pussy would get wet for him. I'd never had this type of experience before and I was nervous as hell because this was my only chance to find a way out.

Get your shit together. You're a bad bitch and you can do anything you put your mind to, I thought to myself. After giving myself a pep talk, I finally walked out of the room. I didn't bother about wrapping a towel around me because I didn't see the point. I knew what I was going in this room to do, so it was time for me to put my big girl panties on. Jonah was already sitting on the edge of the bed jacking his dick. Looking at him disgusted me. I couldn't believe that was the same dick I used to enjoy sucking and cumming all over.

I climbed in the bed and he immediately hovered over me. I prayed he didn't try to kiss me because I didn't want to throw up in his mouth. Instead of him trying to kiss me on my lips, he went straight to my lower region and tongue kissed those lips. I laid there and allowed him to do his thing.

"Act like you want this shit Paris, or the deal is off," he demanded.

"Okay, I'm sorry baby, that shit feels real good, don't stop," I fake moaned as I gripped the back of his head like I normally would do. I closed my eyes and I thought about Draco the entire time he was eating my pussy, in hopes that it would make me cum faster so we could get this shit over with. It only took about another five minutes before I started cumming his mouth.

"That's what the fuck I'm talking about. You missed me eating that pussy?" he asked as he came up for air.

"Yes baby," I lied. I prayed to God my poker face was on point. It must've been because he didn't say anything else before sliding his dick inside of me. I closed my eyes to keep myself from crying. I didn't want to look at his face. I guess the saying was true. No matter how good the sex was when y'all were together, once the feelings were gone so was the passion in sex. This was some of the worst sex I'd ever had. I guess it was because I could still count on one hand how many men I'd allowed to fuck, because sex has a lot to do with emotions and feelings for me. I knew people would think I was a ho for getting pregnant by a married man, but Draco was the third man that could say he knew what this pussy felt like. I was laying here finally realizing how Stony felt in *Set It Off* when she was fucking Nate. I was in a motherfucking bind. After what seemed like hours, which was probably only twenty minutes, Jonah came. He had the nerve to actually nut inside of me. I was so damn glad that I can't have any more kids because I'd have to be on suicide watch if I got pregnant by his ass. I couldn't get up and run to the bathroom fast enough to pee. Once I was finished releasing my bladder, I climbed back in the shower and scrubbed my body until my skin and body was burning. I didn't give a fuck how much it hurt, I just needed to not feel or smell Jonah on my body.

I finished up my shower and this time I moisturized my body and put on clothes. By the time I made it back to the bedroom it was empty but the bedroom door was open. I smiled for the first time that day seeing that. Niggas were always suckers for pussy.

I walked out of the room and all I could see were trees outside, which meant we were in the middle of nowhere. I walked around until I found Jonah standing in the kitchen.

"Cook us something to eat. The kids' room is across the hall. I need to take a nap after that nut. Have dinner ready and be ready for round two when I wake up. Don't even think about trying to leave because you won't know how to get away and there's alarms on all the doors," he advised me before going back to my room. Little did he know, I wasn't going to try to escape. I mean, how far could I actually get with two kids? All I needed to do was get to his phone, which was sitting right here on the counter. I started cooking to play it off. After about twenty minutes I went and peeked in the room to make sure he was sleep. I made sure to put it on him good so he'd be out for at least an hour like always. I crept back in the kitchen and hurriedly dialed Draco's number.

"Whoever the fuck this is better have answers!" he barked into the phone.

"Dray, I don't have a long time to talk. I'm about to send you my location. Please hurry and don't call this number back," I told him before hanging up. I didn't give him a chance to say anything because I couldn't afford to get caught. I texted my location to Draco then deleted my text and phone call. From the looks of it we were two hours from where Draco was. I could finally breathe because in a couple hours, I'd be free. I knew I could have called the police and been out of the situation a lot faster, but the police wouldn't make Jonah pay the way Draco would. I needed that nigga to suffer before taking his last breath for doing what he did to me. I got right back to cooking like I didn't just help Jonah sign his own death certificate.

Chapter 17
Draco

Day after day that turned into nights and weeks as I searched for Paris and the twins but ended up with dead ends. My entire being was in overdrive. I was ready to flip the entire fucking state upside down to find them. Jonah really didn't realize the sleeping beast he had awakened in me. He'd better be counting his fucking days because his demise was near soon as I got to him.

I knew Paris was scared out of her mind because she didn't really know this nigga. Fuck, I didn't know his bitch ass was a real-life psych patient until Sasha broke the shit down to me. He was capable of any and everything he became fixated on, and I knew for sure Paris and my twins were it. The only positive thing was that I knew he wouldn't bring any harm to them because he loved them and was in love with Paris, but I still couldn't trust it. Deep down in his deranged heart, he knew Paris wasn't in love with him and that alone would make the sanest man insane. But a part of me still didn't trust that nigga.

I was losing it. I couldn't eat, drink, shit, or piss as the days went by. Only time I got up from the fucking sofa was to retrieve another bottle of D'ussé when I finished the previous bottle. Only then did I make use of the bathroom. This shit was stressing me out. I felt lost and out of control, even weak, and I ain't never been a weak nigga. Shit was totally out of my character.

I murdered and tortured niggas for a living. I eliminated threats, and the fact that I couldn't find my little family was killing my soul. I had connections all over the fucking United States and Jonah's bitch ass fell off the grid like he was Harriet Tubman leading the Underground Railroad. I had my hittas Cutta and Hook standing outside my house with assault rifles for security reasons. I wasn't scared, just careful. I didn't trust nobody but those two and myself.

I was out my body behind this entire situation, and I didn't like that shit at all. I thought about going back to Sasha and killing that bitch for giving me the wrong address. That shit led us to acres of fucking land with dirt and grass. I should kill that bitch too, but her karma gone come back strong and if I was lucky, I'd have front row tickets.

I grabbed my phone from the table and turned off the DND. Before then my shit was ringing off the fucking hook from my parents and niggas that I didn't want to talk to. I thought about calling my father to get his people to look into some shit, but he was more ruthless than me. This nigga would have killed everybody in her family until his men found Paris and the twins, but I didn't want that much bloodshed. It would draw too attention to our family, not that my father cared anyway. That nigga would pump lead in a fucking baby if a threat was made against my family or anyone associated with us.

I didn't keep shit from my parents. When I met Paris, I told my father about it and he told me that sugar would turn to shit, but I didn't listen. Paris was too tempting for me to pass up on. He also told me that if I gave Paris the attention that she was seeking, my marriage would be over, and that nigga wasn't lying. I showered Paris with everything she was missing, and I ended up falling in love with her sexy ass. I knew my marriage to Sasha was out of convenience because of our professions, but I was in love with her. Paris swiped all the love that I had in my heart for Sasha the day I saw her.

Bang bang bang bang

I grabbed my .45 and jumped up off the couch at the sound of someone banging on my fucking door. No one knew about this fucking house but the two niggas I had outside who clearly weren't doing their job to let a motherfucker get this close to my property. I swung the door open and the last person I thought to see was staring me in the eyes. I took her in from head to toe. Had this been four years ago, I would have her ass up face down, but this wasn't that and the sight turned my stomach into knots. I put my gun at my waist.

"What the fuck do you want Alana, and what the fuck are you doing here?!" I barked at her. I grabbed the front of her neck, giving it a squeeze. "And how the fuck do you know where I stay, bitch?!" I yanked her neck like a rag doll, waving it from left to right.

"We had an agreement, Draco, and you are not holding your end of the bargain up," she tried to say, but I applied pressure with my thumb to her neck.

"Bitch, I don't care about an agreement! I ain't fucking you no more and Sasha knows everything, so there's nothing you can fucking tell her, so get the fuck off my doorstep." I pushed her and she fell back on her ass. I wanted to laugh, but I was pissed that this bitch was in my presence. I watched as she dragged herself away from me and my niggas laughed. I kicked her in the ass as she crawled away. I looked out the window and made sure her dumbass had left. I turned to look at the two that thought shit was funny.

"And where the fuck was y'all fucking antennas when that crazy bitch pulled up and had the audacity to knock on my door?" I asked them, and the laughter stopped.

"My bad, Boss. I thought she knew you and wanted to give you some live entertainment." This time I laughed as I walked back in my house and slammed the door. For a quick moment, my mind had shifted to something else, but when I sat down on the sofa and looked up at the big ass picture of Paris carrying our babies from her maternity photoshoot, I got pissed off all over again. I grabbed the bottle of D'ussé and fell back on the sofa with the bottle to my mouth. My phone vibrating jarred my daydream. I looked down at the screen and noticed it was an unknown number. I let it ring a few times before I finally picked up.

"Whoever the fuck this is better have answers!" I barked into the phone. Silence. I was about to disconnect the phone when I heard a tiny voice.

"Dray, I don't have a long time to talk. I'm about to send you my location. Please hurry and don't call this number back," she sobbed, and the call disconnected. I couldn't get a fucking word in and that infuriated me even more. I couldn't wait on the location to come through because my nerves were on edge, so I sprang into action and sprinted to my room. I was already dressed. All I had to do was slip my feet into my black Timbs. I lifted my mattress that held everything from a mac 11 to a .40. I chose to take two .45s and put them in my waistband.

I was going to shoot him if he got out of line, but I had something special for his bitch ass. I walked out my room and out the door with my hittas following close behind me. No words needed to be spoken because they already knew what it was. I looked down at my phone and noticed that the location was about two hours out from where we were. We hopped in the Tahoe and pulled off to the address. We turned that two-hour drive into an hour and a half.

"Make this shit easy, in and out. Get my girl and my kids and let me handle the rest," I told them as they killed the lights when we pulled up. Jonah thought he was smart coming this far away like I wouldn't find his bitch ass. I felt stupid for not looking further.

"We got you, Boss. Get yo' girl and the babies and you got the rest," they repeated to me as we got out the truck.

It was a nice house, almost family like, just not my fucking family. I gave the signal for them to go around back because I was kicking the fucking front door down. Fuck being silent. That nigga wasn't being silent when he kidnapped my family. When I heard the back door creak open, I knew they were inside. I waited ten minutes before I walked up the steps and kicked the door in.

The door fell to the ground as I walked in. I didn't see anyone in the foyer, so I made my way to the living room. I noticed a gun and snatched it, putting it in my back pocket. Knowing Jonah, that was probably the only gun he had. As I got further into the living room, I noticed two bassinets and baby shit everywhere. I looked up and noticed Paris frozen in place with both babies in her arms. I could tell she was about to scream, but I put my finger to my lips for her to remain quiet. I noticed my boys behind her and nodded my head. One grabbed her arm and the other took the babies and their bags and left how they entered. Before Paris walked away, she blew a kiss at me and nodded her head toward the steps, telling me that Jonah was there. I nodded my head back and mouthed 'I love you' before they took her and my babies to safety.

"What the fuck was that noise, Paris? I told you if you tried to leave me I would kill us all," I heard Jonah say as he stepped down the steps. I waited for that nigga to hit the last step before I started to laugh.

"Nigga, you really thought I wasn't gon' find her? You thought that you were gonna get the last fucking laugh?" I taunted him, and he tried to run to the foyer to get his gun. "Nah nigga, I got that in my back pocket," I told him, because I knew he was going for his gun.

"Nigga, fuck you. You fucked up my sister's life but you not about to fuck up mine," he said like I didn't have both my guns pointed to his head. The lil' nigga did have heart.

"Yeah nigga, you right. I ain't gon' fuck up your life, I'm 'bout to take that bitch," I told him before Hook hit him from behind, knocking his ass out.

"Bring that nigga to the dungeon. It's time to have some fun," I told Hook, walking past him and out the door to the truck.

After I got Paris and the kids squared away at my crib, I went to my warehouse that Hook brought Jonah to. I walked in and dapped up some of the homies and went downstairs to the basement. I almost vomited in my mouth at the smell that permeated the air. I grabbed my mask to cover my nose and mouth and put on my gloves and overalls. I grabbed my baby machete and walked over to Jonah's bloody body. They did a number on him, but I told them not to touch his face and they listened.

"Tell me you sorry, nigga," I told him as I turned my machete.

"Fuck you, nigga. I don't get on my knees for no nigga." I was surprised to hear the nigga talk like that. Maybe he did have a little hood in him. I had him hanging in the air butt ass naked with chains around his wrists. A light puddle of blood was at his feet from his flesh wounds.

"I promised Sasha that I wouldn't kill yo' bitch ass but I see you got a lot of mouth, so I will do you an even greater favor." I looked at him as he eyed me suspiciously.

"And what's that, motherfucker?" he asked with bass in his voice that made me chuckle.

"Not cut yo' motherfucking head off so that yo' ugly ass momma can give you a proper burial," I told him and then proceeded to cut his body into pieces. When I was finished with him, only his head and arms were still intact. That should teach any nigga a lesson to not fuck with what's mine.

Chapter 18
Sasha

It'd been almost two months since Draco came here claiming Jonah kidnapped Paris and his twins. I wasn't lying when I told Draco I didn't know where my brother was. I did give him the wrong address though. I wasn't about to help Draco kill my brother. I just knew Draco was going to come hurt me after he found out that was just an empty lot, but he never showed up.

It wasn't until last month that I realized Paris and the twins were living with Draco at his new spot. I had hired a private investigator to find out where he lived. I was given pictures of him, her, and the kids leaving in and out of his building like one big happy family. That explained why he never came back to the house looking for Jonah. It didn't explain where my brother was though.

I didn't want Draco to know that I knew where he lived, so I had been going to the shop so I could talk to him, but he was never there. My brother wouldn't just disappear like this or go without calling me for this long period of time. Even when Draco was searching for Paris, Jonah was reaching out to me. I asked him about her and he claimed he didn't know where she was. I couldn't tell if he was lying or not. Now that he'd disappeared, I wasn't too sure.

I'd been going to the shop so I could talk to Draco, but whenever I went he was never there. I didn't know if he took off time to help Paris with the kids or what. I was trying not to let him know that I knew where he lived, but I couldn't take this anymore. I needed answers about my brother now.

I took a quick shower and got dressed in a pair of blue jean shorts, a white tank top, and a pair of sandals. I combed out my sew-in and applied a light coat of makeup. I gave myself the once over then grabbed my keys and purse leaving the house. Draco lived about thirty minutes away from me. When I pulled up I was surprised by the neighborhood he lived in. He always lived on the expensive side of town. I entered his building and, of course, I couldn't go straight up. I had to check in at the front desk.

"Hello, how can I help you, Miss?"

"I'm here to see Draco Turner. I'm his sister from out of town and I'm trying to surprise him."

"I'm sorry, but we're not allowed to give out our residents' information. I would have to call upstairs first."

I sighed because I felt defeated. What if I allowed her to call upstairs and he said I can't come up? Then all of this would have been for nothing. I didn't have any other choice though, and I knew I couldn't bribe her because it wouldn't be worth her job.

"Okay, can you let him know that Sasha Turner is here?"

"Sure, give me one moment."

My nerves were all over the place while I waited for her to make the phone call. After a couple of minutes, she gave me the apartment number. The doorman swiped his badge and I got on the elevator taking it up the top floor, which was the penthouse. I didn't know why he would pay all this money for a condo and not buy a house.

I stepped off the elevator and walked up to his door. I was about to knock but it was swung open to a furious Draco. He had a scowl on his face so ugly that if looks could kill, I'd be dead where I stood.

"What the fuck are you doing here, Sasha?" Draco bellowed.

"I came to talk to you about something important. Can I come in?" I asked.

Draco looked at me then behind him, debating on if he should let me in or not.

"She can come in," I heard Paris say from behind him.

Draco stepped to the side and I walked inside of his house. It was beautifully decorated and looked nothing like our old place. I could already tell that Paris has something to do with the décor. There was a maternity picture on the wall with her alone then another one with him in the picture. Looking at that shit caused my eyes to water. My husband had actually been living a double life right under my nose. He was actually there for that bitch during her pregnancy just as much as my brother was, and that amazed me.

"Okay, you're in. Now what do you want?" Draco asked.

My eyes darted over to Paris sitting on the couch with the twins. I was hoping that I could talk to Draco in private. I had been prolonging our divorce, but seeing Draco here with her and his kids, I knew it was over. I couldn't compete with her before the kids, and I was married to him, so I knew I can't compete with her now. I'd been doing a lot of thinking lately and I wondered if I would have just given in and had kids would things have turned out different between me and Draco. Would he have been so busy loving on me and our kids that he wouldn't have looked in Paris's direction? Like, I'm successful and beautiful. I had a lot to bring to the table and any man would be lucky to have me in his life, yet I was busy doubting myself. I needed these questions answered before I parted ways with Draco for good.

"I was hoping that we could talk in private. This is kind of personal," I told him.

The look on his face made me regret even letting those words come out of my mouth.

"Da fuq you mean can we talk in private? You came to my house uninvited, and you expect me to send my woman to another room so we can talk?" he asked as if he was shocked by the audacity of my question.

"Wow, you're a piece of work, Draco. After all the shit that we've been through and what I've put up with, I can't get a few minutes of your time? You're actually going to throw your relationship with this bitch in my face? We're not even officially divorced yet."

"Who the fuck you calling a bitch? Don't let my looks and size fool you because I'll beat your ass and not bat an eye. Be glad that I'm holding my babies right now," Paris jumped in.

"Yo, Sasha, chill out with that disrespectful shit before I kick your ass out. You will respect her in my house. Whether you like it or not, Paris is my family. We're only still married because you're dragging your feet with our proceedings," Draco added.

"I'm sorry, Draco, this shit is just irritating, and I don't know how to handle it," I confessed.

"Come help me take them to their room then you can talk to her in private," Paris said.

"Are you sure? You don't have to leave. She can say whatever it is in front of you or get the fuck out," he assured her.

"I'm sure, it's time for their nap anyway," she replied.

Draco walked away from me without saying a word. He

whispered something in Paris's ear that caused her to smile from ear to ear before they walked away to another part of the house.

I sat down on the couch waiting for Draco to return. I assumed he was helping put the twins to bed until I heard Paris giggling followed by moaning. Tears instantly escaped my eyes because never did I think Draco would be this damn disrespectful to me. He was actually in there fucking her knowing that I was right here in the front. It wasn't like they were being discreet, so that meant he didn't care about me hearing.

After sitting there for almost fifteen minutes, Draco walked in the front fixing his clothes. I wanted to punch him in his shit. The sight of him really disgusted me.

"Ugh, I can't believe I ever loved your bitch ass," I said the closer he got to me.

"Sasha, don't get hit in your shit. We both know there's no bitch in my blood and if that be the case, I can't believe I ever loved your ho ass. You have ten minutes so get to talking. You're interrupting our alone time."

I was about to go off on his ass but that wasn't going to get us anywhere, so I took a deep breath to calm down before speaking.

"Look, I didn't come here to fight with you, Draco. I came to find out where my brother is."

"Why the hell would I know where that nigga at? I don't fuck with him."

"Come on now, Draco, don't play dumb with me. You came to my house with a gun looking for Jonah because you claimed he took Paris and the twins, but now they're here and my brother is nowhere to be found. Did you kill my brother, Draco?"

"What? Why the fuck would you ask me some shit like that for?"

"I just explained to you why."

"That was a misunderstanding. Paris went back to New Orleans to visit her family and let them see the twins. The situation between me, her, and Jonah was becoming too stressful, and she needed a break. After being gone for two weeks, she called and told me where she was and I went to get my family. There was no way in hell I was going to allow her to raise my kids in a different state away from me," Draco explained.

I looked at Draco and couldn't believe how he could lie with such a straight face. I hadn't heard shit about her having a family all this time since she'd been out here, now all of a sudden she took her newborn babies and left the state. The way Draco made it seem, she had no support and he was the only one in her corner.

"Come on, Draco, if you killed my brother please tell me where his body is so we can have some closure. You already shot me and Jayce. This is the least you could do."

"Man, gone somewhere with this dumb ass shit. Why the fuck you keep asking me did I kill his ass? I already told you no. Are you wearing a wire or some shit? You trying to get me locked up?" Draco asked as he started patting me down.

"What are you doing? I'm not wearing a damn wire. Me and my parents are just worried about Jonah. He's never went this long without talking to us. I just need to know what's going on. I'm begging you, Draco, if you know what's going on, tell me," I pleaded as tears fell from my eyes.

"I'm sorry, Sasha, but I can't help you. If he tries to reach out to Paris, I'll call and let you know."

"Really? This is some bullshit and you know it, Draco. It's cool though, I know that you'll never incriminate yourself or your boys. You don't even have to say anything. If he's alive, just let him go. I'll make sure he doesn't tell anyone. If he's dead, just leave his body where someone can find him."

"Okay, your time's up. I'm not about to keep discussing this with you," Draco said as he walked me to the door.

"Alright, can I ask you one question? After this, I'll be out of your life for good. I won't fight with you and we can go forward with the divorce proceedings."

"What's up? Ask your question."

"If I would have given you a child, do you think things would be different between us? I mean, why wasn't I enough for you?"

Draco ran his hand across his face like my question had further irritated him.

"Look Sasha, I can't dwell on the what ifs right now. I can't say whether if we had kids it would have changed things or not. I mean, it probably wouldn't have stopped me from cheating on you with Paris, but I doubt things would have gotten as serious between us. The truth is we started growing apart. We both knew it and that's how we found our way in other people's beds. It's best we leave the past where it is and focus on our future with other people."

"You're right, I won't cause y'all any problems," I told him before walking out of his house and to my car. There was no need for me to bitch and moan about the situation because it wasn't going to change anything. I would be the one miserable while he was having the time of his life.

I sat in my car for a good five minutes crying my eyes out. Reality finally had hit me. My marriage was over and I was positive that my brother was dead. There's no purpose of Draco keeping him alive. I knew Draco, and if Jonah really did take Paris and those kids, Draco wasn't going to spare him. I didn't want to be alone so I decided to call Jayce.

"Hello," he answered after the third ring.

"Hey, I was wondering if you wanted to come over to my

place. I could really use someone to talk to right now. Everything in my life is fucked up right now."

"What's wrong?"

"I would rather we talked in person," I replied.

"I can't do that, Sasha. I love my wife and I told her that if she didn't kick me out I'd end things with you."

"Really? You disrupted my motherfucking life now it's just fuck me?"

"The fuck you mean I disrupted your life? You allowed me to fuck you and that's all it was. I never promised to love you or give you a new life. It's not my fault you got caught by your husband and he left your ass. If anything, you fucked my life up. I damn near got killed because of you, and my wife wouldn't have found out about our affair if that wasn't for you either."

"Wow, that's how you feel Jhayce?"

"Yes, it is, please don't contact me again because I'm going to block your ass. You won't be seeing me again either because I put in a transfer," he said before hanging up the phone on me.

I sat there not believing Jhayce had played me. He and Draco had me fucked up. I didn't need either of their asses. I was about to go back to being a cold-hearted bitch. Being in love had me slacking from my work anyway. After all, I had a reputation to keep in the courtroom.

Chapter 19
Paris
One year later

Draco was really a dog ass nigga, but he couldn't have ever played with me the way he did when Sasha came to our home that day. All the fucking moaning and laughing I did while he was fucking me against the door he closed behind us, she had to hear. That's what that bitch got for hiring a PI to spy on us. I bet she thought I didn't know, but I did. Nothing could get past me, so Draco better tread lightly. My mother once told me, "how you get him is how you lose him," but that shit was a myth. I didn't believe in that shit and Draco wasn't trying to lose his life.

After the shit Sasha pulled, Draco didn't trust her so he uprooted us and now we lived in the middle of Timbuk-fucking-tu where nobody could find us. The home was beautiful and he let me decorate it to my liking. It was a five-bedroom, four-bathroom home with too much space. Half the house was still not decorated but the important parts were. The only thing I couldn't touch was his mancave. My only request was that he put a stripper pole in it, and he was more than happy to agree. We used it a couple of times until I was too tired to climb up and down it.

We had to go at least twenty miles to get to the city, which was fine with me. I was currently working from home because Draco refused to hire a nanny. He didn't trust anyone with his kids outside of us. When he went away on business, he took us with him, per usual. He was a very active father and I loved that about him. He didn't leave me to take care of the twins by myself.

The only thing he couldn't help with was the breastfeeding. He gave them baths, changed diapers, and he even took them out just so I could have me time to get pampered. Draco was everything I needed but didn't know I deserved, if that made sense. He gave them more attention than he did me and I was starting to get jealous. He'd even relocated his shop, keeping the same workers but hiring a dude to control the front counter because I told him it couldn't be a bitch.

He was also currently looking for another building in New York and California to branch out and expand. He was still in the streets but not as heavy, but I always told him that as long as he made it back to me at the end of the day, I was good. I think that's where Sasha fucked up at. I accepted Draco for who he was and what he did from the beginning. I never tried to change how he got his money or my position in his life. If he wanted to change, that was a decision he and God would have to make.

Let us not forget about that Alana bitch. He told me all about her surprise visit and how he threatened her to not let him see her again. I had a feeling the bitch wasn't fully out the picture because she was one of those bitches that liked to be seen. But what she didn't know about me was I moved in silence. Just like Draco had hittas, so did I, but he didn't know that because mine were behind the scenes. One call and that bitch would become a memory. I didn't dwell on that shit with

Alana because she ain't want no smoke when we both were fucking Draco.

After Sasha left our condo, a month after that the divorce was final. The bitch tried to get half of everything yelling infidelity because he was fucking with me, but that didn't work. I didn't know what type of lawyer Draco had, but it was a damn good one. There was no evidence of me and him fucking around because Draco had paperwork stating that he served the divorce papers years ago, but Sasha never took it seriously, so he was deemed single in court. That was some Kim and Kanye shit, but I kept my mouth closed.

I begged him to tell me what he did with Jonah's body because I knew he killed him, but he refused to tell me. He always said, "you know what you need to know," and that pissed me off. He got mad, accusing me of stilling wanting the nigga, and I made his ass sleep in the guest room for two weeks. This nigga would lay by the door every night begging me to at least let him see the twins, like he hadn't seen them all day.

One night I was being petty and opened the door naked then sat both my fat ass babies on the floor right next to him, making sure to squat and give him a pussy shot. I laughed as he tried to tackle me to the floor, and the twins crying was what stopped him. I always told him not to question my loyalty because if he did, then why were we together? The shit I went through to be with this nigga would have been in vain.

Once the divorce was final, he wanted us to get married, but I told him no because I didn't want to suffer the same fate as Sasha. I didn't want him to jump out of one marriage and into another without thinking shit through. When I first met Draco, I took shit for what it was. I was his side bitch even though he didn't treat me like it, so I kept my feelings at bay. Over time my feelings developed for him, and I tried to deny it until I got pregnant. Just me knowing I was carrying his babies made me fall in love with him even more.

I fell in love with his scent, his skin, the way he handled his business in and out the bedroom, and just his entire being made me feel at peace. I'd never felt safer in my life like I felt with Draco. We both knew that the babies were his, but I didn't want them to be because he was married, but we were both adults. I couldn't afford to let a married man break me down. I would have ended up on the *First 48* fucking with Draco behind my heart. He understood but didn't like it.

"You still overthinking shit I see. What you staring into space for?" Draco scared the shit outta me as I sat on the sofa. Draco was still fine as fuck dressed in a white tee and gray joggers with his socks and Nike slippers as he walked around the couch and sat down, lifting my feet into his lap. His hair was lined to perfection, and he was letting his beard grow so I could continue to wet it up with my juices. I knew I dozed off but when that nigga left this morning, he was not dressed like that. I kept my mouth closed because he communicated with me about everything on a need-to-know basis. If it was business, he'd tell me later. He massaged my feet as my head fell to the back of the sofa.

"I was just thinking about us Dray, that's all," I told him through the moans.

"What's there to think about?" his angry ass asked. He always got an attitude when I answered him like that. "We got our happy ending even though that ain't what you wanted," he pouted, and I thought it was so cute. That was true. I didn't want to break up his marriage, but he stopped loving Sasha long before I came along.

"Draco, so you not gon' ever tell me what y'all did to that boy's body?" I asked just to get under his skin. He pushed my feet hard as fuck to the floor and I fell with it. I laughed my ass off, but he didn't find shit funny.

"You think that shit funny until I push yo' shit back too." I stopped laughing when he realized his mouth had overtalked his brain. I rolled over and tooted my ass in the air before getting up.

"What you mean too, nigga?" I looked at him shaking his head from left to right. I sat back on the sofa, grabbing my iPad and placing it in my lap. I could tell that he knew he fucked up, and he also knew he wasn't about to get away without telling me what I wanted to know. I put my foot back on his lap and told him to keep fucking rubbing. I didn't care how mad he was, I wanted my feet rubbed. He'd left early this morning and now it was ten at night, which was very odd, but I didn't question him because I didn't have to. If he valued his life, as I stated before, he wouldn't fucking play with me.

"Ok, a nigga was trying to spare yo' dizzy ass the details but since you want the truth, I'mma give it to you, but before I tell you, you gotta sign this NDA. If you speak anything about what I'm about to tell you, I will take full custody of the twins, including the one you got in your fucking belly," he belted out, but I didn't take him serious. I laughed again, but he gave me a look that made me zip my lips. Oh, I forgot to tell y'all. Yes, I am currently five months pregnant with a boy and hopefully not another fucking girl hiding behind him, because my belly was huge this time around too.

"I'm not playing with you 'cuz you too fucking nosey. You saw enough but I forgot with you, it's never enough," he said, reaching into his pocket and pulling out a piece of paper. He grabbed a pen off the table and began to unfold the paper. This nigga was serious. I wasn't the only person that saw some shit. His niggas were there too.

"Did you make your friends sign this shit too?" I asked, kicking him.

"Nah, them niggas work for me. It's what they do for me." He put emphasis on me. I tried to read the paper, but he yanked it from me. "Nah, fuck all that, just sign the shit P so I can tell you what you dying to know." He pushed the pen in my hand, forcing me to sign the document. I wanted to know so bad, and the anticipation was killing me, so I signed the shit and threw it back at him.

"There, now tell me what happened." It was his turn to laugh, but I didn't understand the joke.

"After you left, they brought his bitch ass to my dungeon. When I got there he was beat the fuck up, but my request was for them to not touch his face and wrists. I was only doing that so he could have a proper burial because I respected his family, and the nigga was mentally crazy. I had his ass hanging butt ass naked from the ceiling with chains holding his wrists together. He knew he was about to die, and the nigga was still talking shit. When he mentioned your name, I lost it. I grabbed my machete and cut his ass into little bitty pieces and put his body in the furnace. No face, no case, so now it's fuck his family and their closure."

I didn't recognize the monster before me. He'd turned into another man that I wasn't familiar with, and it must have displayed on my face.

"I told you some shit you don't need to know, but you asked for it. You good?" he asked me like he'd just told me a bedtime story. I was stuck. I didn't know what to say. I mean, I knew he was the plug, but a murderer? Fuck no.

"I know yo' ass ain't scared of me? He had that shit coming because he tried to take what belonged to me all along, so he had to go." His voice was back to normal, and it calmed me and my kicking son.

"See, I knew I shouldn't have told yo' ass shit because you got my son all upset." He looked down at my belly to see the movements. "Come here, Paris," he demanded, but I hesitated at first. He gave me a hard look and I lifted myself and straddled him. He reached up and kissed my lips, showing me that what he did had to be done. His mouth then moved to my neck, licking and biting, and my hips involuntarily rolled against his hard rod.

"Fuck," I heard him moan as my arms wrapped around the back of his neck. His hands grabbed my hips trying to stop me, but he couldn't.

"You got panties on?" he asked me.

"You know I don't." I kissed his lips as he lifted my night-gown over my head. He was lucky I had that on because I hated clothes when I was pregnant.

He reached between us, and I lifted up so he could pull my favorite toy out. He was ready to come and play too. He grabbed my hips and eased me down on his dick, and I sighed in satisfaction. I was about to bounce but he stopped me.

"Don't go crazy on my shit. Ride this big motherfucker nice and slow. I wanna feel everything," he groaned as I slowed my pace and started to circle my hips.

"Damn, just like that. Put them titties in my face and your arms around my neck," he guided. He knew I hated that shit. I was in control and I wanted it to stay that way. I grinded my hips against him as he fucked me back. I was overwhelmed so I fell to his chest, gripping his neck tighter. I felt his hands inter-lock with mine and smiled. I was out my mind as I slow fucked Draco until we both climaxed. I looked up at him as he laughed. I was so tired that I moved back from him and rolled my eyes. I needed a nap after that quickie.

"What the fuck is so funny?" I looked up at him laughing

like I was tickling him. His eyes trailed down my body to my left hand. I looked down and almost passed out.

"No, you didn't!" I tried to jump up, but he held me in place.

"And you don't even have to answer because you signed the marriage license already." He laughed even harder.

"You really thought you signed an NDA? I trust you with my life Paris, and now you are my wife." I tried to push him away as he rained kisses all over my face and chest.

Clearly, I understood the assignment of being his side bitch but he didn't, and now I'm stuck with this nigga for life, so y'all women better watch out for a nigga like Draco, because the real one is already taken.

THE END!!!!!

Also by Kevina Hopkins

Movin' Different 4: A Hood Millionaire Romance

Movin' Different 3: A Hood Millionaire Romance

Movin' Different 2: A Hood Millionaire Romance

Movin' Different: A Hood Millionaire Romance

A Chi-Town Millionaire Stole My Heart

A Chi-Town Millionaire Stole My Heart 2

A Chi-Town Millionaire Stole My Heart 3

King & Armani

King & Armani 2

King & Armani 3

I'm Just Doin' Me

I'm Just Doin' Me 2

Lil Mama A Ryder

Lil Mama A Ryder 2

When A Savage Loves A Woman

When A Savage Loves A Woman 2

The Autobiography Of A Capo's Wife

Every Dope Boy Got A Side Chick

Also By Miss. Jazzie

The Wife Of A Certified Henchman 3

The Wife Of A Certified Henchman 2

When The Side B*tch Understands The Assignment

The Wife Of A Certified Henchman

Magnolia & Dior 2: A Hood Love Story

Magnolia & Dior: A Hood Love Story

Married To The Don Of New Orleans

Married To The Don Of New Orleans 2

Married To The Don Of New Orleans 3

A Nolia Boss Saved Me

A Nolia Boss Saved Me 2

A Nolia Boss Saved Me 3